THE LIES BETWEEN US

CYNTHIA COOKE

The Lies Between Us
Deadly Secrets Book 4

By
USA Today Bestselling Author
Cynthia Cooke

Copyright © 2020 by
Cynthia Cooke. All rights reserved.

This book is a work of fiction. Names, characters, places, and incidents are the product of the author's imagination or are used fictitiously. Any resemblance to actual events, locales, or person, living or dead, is coincidental. This book is published by Cynthia Cooke of state of North Carolina. This book / ebook is licensed for your personal enjoyment only. All rights reserved. No part of this publication may be reproduced, stored in a retrieval system, or transmitted in any form or by any means, electronic, mechanical, recording or otherwise, without the prior written permission of the author.

Contact:
Cynthia@CynthiaCooke.com
Newsletter Bookbub Amazon Website Twitter Facebook Pinterest

1

Tom Phillips pocketed the picture of the brunette with a million-dollar smile and stunning green eyes. She was beautiful, magazine perfect, and yet there was a hint of vulnerability in her eyes that reached out and grabbed hold of him, compelling him to want to help her. But could he trust her?

He couldn't stop wondering what her story was. How did she get involved with a man like Bodega? Why risk her life by working with the FBI? Or was she setting him up? At her request, their conversations and this meeting were off the books. No one knew about the op but his partner Sam and their boss out of the NY office. He was taking a huge risk, but if he could nail Carlos Bodega, it would be worth it.

"What can I get you?" the bartender asked. At this time of the afternoon the room was practically empty. There was a woman sitting in a booth by herself, a slew of papers and an open computer in front of her, and a man in a suit nursing a beer and watching the news on the TV screen hanging on the wall.

Tom tapped his fingers on the long mahogany bar and looked up at the array of top-shelf bottles lining the wall. "Scotch on the rocks." He glanced at his watch as the bartender placed the drink in front of him. Mrs. Bodega should be there within ten minutes. Tom took his drink to a table in front of the window so he could watch the street. He quickly made note of the cars parked out front, which pedestrians were on the move, and which were just hanging around.

He'd been talking to Anita Bodega for weeks. She'd give him bits and pieces, all verified and accurate, but nothing that would be enough to take Carlos down. He needed more. The FBI had been working for years to infiltrate Carlos Bodega's organization, but each time they'd gotten close, he'd slip through their nets.

This might be their first real break but at what cost? What would Anita Bodega want in exchange for giving him the goods to take down her husband? She had to know the risk would be extreme. Her husband had people everywhere.

His phone vibrated. He slipped it out of his pocket and glanced down at the screen. *Cat.* His wife had been expecting him yesterday afternoon. He should answer, tell her he was fine. Tell her everything was okay. But he didn't. He had to admit to himself that he dreaded going home. He'd had a hard time facing her ever since he'd learned Stuart Marsters, infamous head of the

National Counter Terrorist Agency known as the CTA, was her father.

That man had run an organization that dove deep into the shady areas of the intelligence agencies with little regard for rule and the damage they caused. If that wasn't bad enough, her sisters, Genie and Becca Marsters, had thrown in with Josh Cameron. The three of them were running a new CTA offshoot group focused on cleaning up Stuart Martsters' messes. Too little too late, if you asked him.

Tom had kept tabs on their organization ever since he'd learned Emerich, the terrorist that had killed Cat's dad, still targeted the sisters. He wanted to use their abilities. Abilities he still didn't trust or understand. Cat swore to him she wasn't involved, but lately he'd heard whispers the Marsters sisters weren't the only ones with special abilities caused by the CTA's experiments with gene manipulation all those years ago. There were others, and recently Emerich was killed by the group after he was found kidnapping several of Marsters' original subjects.

Tom didn't know how to process that. To come to terms with and accept that his wife had *powers*. How could he trust her? He wasn't even—

"Tom Phillips?" The woman spoke with barely a hint of an accent.

He looked up and blinked slowly. Anita Bodega's picture didn't do her justice. Makeup was flawless, hair perfection. Her clothes and jewelry, expensive. The woman's poise and posture spoke of extreme wealth and the confidence of royalty. He supposed in her world, she was. So why would a woman like her risk everything to help him and the FBI destroy her husband?

He gave a slight nod. "Can I buy you a drink?"

"Patron. On the rocks," she told the bartender as he walked toward them. He nodded and went behind the bar to fix it. She took a seat and leaned across the table. "It's nice to finally meet you." A whiff of expensive perfume reached him.

"I didn't expect it would be at a high-class hotel in San Francisco," Tom said as a man with slicked-back dark hair walked into the room wearing dress pants and a dark jacket. His gaze moved over them as he took a seat at the bar. Tom didn't like the way he watched them through the mirror on the wall.

Mrs. Bodega smiled. "Every month or so I come to the city for a weekend shopping trip. I get bored living in the mountains. I much prefer the energy of the city and it is so beautiful here, is it not?"

"It is. Very beautiful." He looked at her over the rim of his glass and took a sip of his scotch.

Whether the woman knew it or not, the man at the bar was there to keep an eye on her. Either to keep her safe or make sure she stayed in line, Tom could only guess. Carlos Bodega ran one of the three biggest cartels in South America. His reach was worldwide. He wasn't a man to take chances, and he didn't make mistakes.

"These are my sisters." Anita took out a photo of

two young women, also stunningly beautiful, and pushed it across the table toward him. "They're both brilliant, attractive, and attending Columbia University in New York. When you can prove to me they are safe and can't be touched, I will give you what you want."

He frowned. "They are safe. Right now. Why put them in jeopardy?"

He watched her eyes as he asked the question; they usually told more than any words spoken.

"I overheard Carlos on the phone. He has plans for them. He wants them in his organization and has already been grooming Sarah." She pointed to one of the girls in the picture. "The boy she's dating is loyal to Carlos. He's been teaching her...things."

"I'm sorry." Tom shook his head. Men like Carlos had no respect for family, for people, for life. All he wanted was power.

"I wasn't given a choice when I was forced to marry Carlos. My father worked with him. I became his property when I turned eighteen. Their arrangement didn't include Savannah and Sarah. My sisters were supposed to be off-limits. But for all I know, my father is indebted to him again."

Tom pushed back his chair. "I'll have it done by tonight."

"Thank you. You'll let me know when? I'm in the penthouse." She passed a keycard across the table that would allow him to reach the penthouse floor from the elevators.

He saw the man's eyes in the mirror follow the

movement. He pocketed the card. "You'll be hearing from me. Watch your back. You have an admirer."

He gestured toward the man at the bar. She turned and looked at him, her face visibly going pale.

"You all right?"

Her smile trembled on her lips. "Yes. Thank you."

He got up and left the bar. He had work to do.

2

CAT PHILLIPS PULLED in a deep breath and tried not to panic. How many times had Tom been late from a meeting, a business trip? *Many times.* So why was she so worried this time? When he hadn't returned her call yesterday, she wasn't worried. They often went days without speaking when he was away on business. So why did she have this nagging feeling in the corner of her brain that something was wrong?

She tried to call the hotel directly, but the phone in his room just rang. She bit her lip and called his colleague, Sam, who she'd met at a Christmas party last year. Feeling slightly ridiculous, she apologized for bothering him and told him there was a small problem at the house and she couldn't get in touch with her husband. Not a big lie, there was a problem. She was about to go into a full-blown panic. Sam assured her he was with Tom at the conference and that they had decided to stay another day. He'd make sure Tom gave her a call as soon as he found him.

She thanked Sam and hung up the phone. He'd been one of the first people she'd met after they relocated to New York from Reno. He'd assured her everything was fine. So why didn't she believe him?

She made herself a cup of tea and tried to relax, waiting for either Sam or Tom to call her back. When an hour had passed and she hadn't heard from either of them, she picked up the phone again and dialed her sister.

"Becca, I need you and Genie," she said, her voice shaking. She hoped she wasn't panicking over nothing; if she was, she trusted Becca and Genie to tell her.

"Genie's here with me," Becca said. "I'll put you on speaker."

They were triplets, and after what happened last year when Daddy died, they each knew no matter how much time they spent apart, each of them would drop whatever was happening to be there for the other. It was an unspoken truth, and Cat knew she could count on them.

"I'm here, what is it?" Genie asked.

"It's Tom. I think...he's gone."

"What do you mean, he's gone?" Becca demanded, her voice sharp.

"He went out of town for work," Cat said. "He was only supposed to be gone for a few days, but he didn't come home when he was supposed to. I called the hotel and he never checked out. A co-worker says he's still there, but I can't reach him, and it's been two days." She sat at the table, thankful Mark and Annie were at school and she had the house to herself.

"Did you look for him?" Becca asked. "I mean *really* look?"

"No, Becca," Cat said, annoyed. She was expecting the question, but it didn't make it any easier to hear. "I turned *it* off. I had to in order to save my marriage. Tom didn't take hearing about us—about what we can do—well. He needs time. That's why I'm calling you. Why I need your help to find him. Or to tell me to stop worrying and that everything is okay."

"For God's sake, Cat. Turn it back on," her sister Becca yelled through the phone line. "If you have a feeling Tom's in trouble, then you need to listen to it."

Cat pulled the phone away from her ear and scowled, her heart dropping in defeat. Becca was right. She knew that, but it didn't make it any easier to hear. "It's not that easy. I made a promise."

"To who?" Becca asked.

"To Tom. After Daddy and everything that happened..." After a terrorist murdered their father and almost killed all three of them, she promised she would turn it off and never mention it again. Not only for their sake, but for Mark and Annie's too.

"Cat, you know we can't do this for you. You're going to have to do it," Genie said, always the reasonable sister.

"I don't think I can," Cat admitted, her voice shredding through the phone.

"Cat, you've got this," Genie said, her voice firm but gentle. "You've done it before."

"No, Genie, you don't understand. I don't *got* this. I'm a mess. A complete mess." Tears flooded her eyes.

"You're doing fine," Genie said. "Where are Mark and Annie?"

"At school."

"Good. Call Tom's mom and ask if she can watch them for a few days. Becca and I will make a few phone calls and see if we can trace his movements. Where was the last place he was seen?"

"San Francisco. At the Omni. He was there for a conference."

"All right," Genie said. "We are at Dad's—" She paused. "At *our* house on Puget now and will head that way. Get on a plane. We'll meet you at the hotel. Don't worry, Cat. We will find him. Everything will be okay."

"Thank you, Genie," Cat said, feeling much better. "Do you think I'm overreacting? His co-worker said everything was fine."

"What's his name?" Genie asked.

"Sam. Uh…" She looked at their contacts on the computer. "Sam Wagner."

"Okay, I'll look into him too," Genie said. "And Cat, no, I don't think you're overreacting. Becca's right, if your gut is telling you something is wrong, then you need to listen to it."

"Turn *it* back on," Becca said. "I warned you something wasn't quite right with Tom. That he wasn't on the up and up."

"Becca!" Cat heard Genie admonish. But what could Cat say? Becca was right. She knew Tom was hiding something too, and if she were honest with herself, she'd known for a very long time.

"I'm right and you both know it," Becca said. "For the sake of my niece and nephew, who I haven't seen in way too long, I want you to turn your abilities back on, pronto."

"I will. I promise." Cat cringed as she said the words. The truth was, it wasn't her promise to Tom that kept her from turning her abilities back on; it was because she'd been afraid. As much as she hated to admit it, there was something off with her husband. Now she would be forced to face it, whether she was ready to or not.

"Good. We'll see you soon." Becca disconnected the line.

Cat entered Mark's room and pulled his Spiderman suitcase from the top of the closet and started to pack his bags. Luckily, Tom's mom was home and would love to have the kids. She set the packed bags by the front door, knowing her mother-in-law's driver would pick them up before getting the kids from school. She drove to the airport and two hours later was on the way to San Francisco.

3
———

TOM HAD BEEN DRIVING for most of the day, following the black SUV through the city, across the Golden Gate, and into the mountains heading north. Carlos had a compound in California's coastal mountain range, but they'd yet to discover where. He fell back out of sight several times as the highway dwindled to a two-lane road that curved through the mountains.

There was a fine line between staying so far back he wasn't noticed, and yet not too far enough behind that he wouldn't lose sight of the SUV when it turned off the main highway. After making arrangements for Mrs. Bodega's sisters' protection, he'd gone to her room with the proof she'd wanted that they were safe. He found the room empty—an overturned cup of still warm coffee the only sign of a struggle.

Luckily, the girl at the desk had been concerned when it appeared Mrs. Bodega was upset and had paid attention to the vehicle they left in, even jotting down the license plate number. Didn't take long for the local PD to find the SUV for him. Unfortunately, as they climbed higher into the mountains, he lost his cell service.

Sam and a few others in their New York office were the only ones following his progress. Carlos had eyes everywhere, and they couldn't chance he'd discover Anita was about to turn on him. But it looked like he might already have.

There was something about the haunted look in Anita's eyes, the fear hiding behind the bravado that kept him moving forward. Kept the SUV in his sights. He only hoped Sam wouldn't call in the cavalry and read in the SF office. At least not yet.

He thought of Cat. She would be wondering why he didn't make it home last night. He should have called her, but he'd been up all night making arrangements for Anita's sisters. Extracting two college girls without being noticed was no small feat.

The SUV turned off the mountain road they'd been climbing since leaving the highway and disappeared down a long drive. He couldn't chance following and continued up the mountain until he could find a place to turn off and go in on foot. Odds were there would be cameras along the drive. Carlos had many enemies, law enforcement being one of them.

Tom parked the Range Rover on the side of the road, dropped the keys under the mat, placed his gun in his ankle holster, and headed out on foot through the woods in the direction of where he'd last seen the

SUV. He had to get close enough to the house to see if Anita was in trouble, and how many guards there were. Once he got the info, he'd get back down the hill and call Sam with his location and ask for backup.

If she was in trouble.

And if she wasn't? He could blow this whole op.

He glanced at his watch. By now Cat would have put the kids to bed and would be wondering where he was. Sam would cover for him. He pulled out his phone, turned on the compass app, then headed down the mountain.

He entered a grove of redwoods, thinking how peaceful it was, and focused on nature's rhythm—the sounds of the forest, hoping he'd notice anything out of the ordinary. He followed deer paths, moving through giant ferns and dense brush as hours clicked by and still no estate in sight. He hadn't even caught sight of the drive yet. His stomach roiled. Frustrated, he considered heading back to the Range Rover and to the nearest hotel to wait for Anita to contact him.

If she could contact him.

In the four years Tom had been working in the drug unit, they'd barely made a dent. As soon as one drug kingpin would fall, another would take his place. If Anita was telling the truth about what she had on her husband, and how damaging it could be to his organization, then they finally had the chance to make a real difference. He sure hoped so. He'd seen firsthand the damage this monster could do. Not to mention the countless lives destroyed by the drugs he brought into this country, and the guns and people he trafficked.

But it was hard to keep secrets from spouses. He knew that better than anyone. He'd been an FBI agent before he met Cat, before they fell in love and married. She never had a clue. As an undercover agent, constantly changing his identity from one persona to the next, it was nice to come home and just be Tom, the boring pharmaceutical salesman.

But when he found out who her father was, who her sisters were and what they could do, he was certain she'd discover his secret. Luckily, she hadn't. Either that, or she was a better liar than him. His days of relaxing at home were over. He couldn't enjoy his family. Not anymore. Not now that he knew how easy it would be for Cat to see inside his thoughts, to know what he was thinking and how he really felt.

He liked his thoughts being his own. Maybe that was why he hadn't called her. Maybe he was tired of pretending.

He heard voices and slowed, skirting behind a redwood. He ducked down and peered through the bushes. Two men in forest fatigues were up ahead. He listened to their quiet chatter as they moved down the mountain toward the estate. They mentioned the poor Señora.

As soon as they were out of earshot, he stepped out of the bushes and followed, careful not to get too close as they moved noisily down the mountain, picking out a word every now and then about the Señor heading to New York.

New York. He must have found out about the arrangements Tom made for Anita's sisters. He'd been so careful. Only a few people in the agency were working with him on moving them to a safe house. He had to talk to Sam. To make sure the girls were out of harm's way. He pivoted and started back up the mountain toward the Range Rover, checking his cell once more. Still no service.

He hurried as fast as he dared, but only made it a short way when he heard a crackling sound over one of the guard's radios. *Close.* He crouched down. A twig snapped. He reached for his gun.

"Hold it right there." Tom looked up into the barrel of a rifle. The owner of the gun smiled down at him. "Got you."

4

"According to the woman at the front desk, Tom left early this morning," Cat told her sisters as they entered her husband's hotel suite with their partners, Kyle Montgomery and Josh Cameron, the head of the CTA. They poked around the room, looking in the closet and dresser drawers.

"I thought you said Tom was a pharmaceutical salesman," Kyle asked as Cameron's phone rang.

Cameron walked toward the window as he answered. "Cameron here. What do you have for me?"

"He is," Cat told Kyle and pointed at the three suits hanging in the closet. "He was here for a conference."

Becca pulled a briefcase from the bottom of the closet and set it on the desk. She slid open the locks, emptied the papers, then frowned as she ran her fingers over the bottom of the case. She hit a lever and a false bottom popped open. She pulled out a pistol and a box of ammo. "Since when do salesmen need Glock 45 handguns?"

Cat's eyes widened. "I've never seen that before."

"Thanks, Steve." Cameron hung up the phone and turned to Cat, a look of regret on his face. "Tom said he was here for a pharmaceutical conference?"

"Yes." She picked up a folder from the desk, along with a tote bag and wire-bound conference schedule. All with the logo of the conference emblazoned across their fronts.

"I had one of my people check their website. There are only two photos of Tom at the conference, and both were doctored," Cameron said.

Cat stilled. "What are you saying?"

"I'm saying, Tom didn't attend the conference, but he sure went through a lot of trouble to make it look like he did."

Cat dropped the conference folder. "Well, it wasn't for my benefit. I've never looked for him online. Not once. I've been married to him for ten years. I trust him completely."

"That was a mistake," Becca blurted and held up the gun.

Cat glared at her sister. "You know—"

"Not helping," Genie said, interrupting. "Let's focus on the problem at hand before digging up new ones."

Becca's lips twisted and it was obvious she was holding back from saying what she really thought. Cat turned away. Maybe she was an idiot. "If Tom wasn't here for the conference, then why was he here, and better yet, where is he now?"

"There's only one way to find out." Becca walked toward her, reaching for her hand.

Cat stared at it. She knew what Becca wanted. She just wasn't sure she was ready.

Genie touched her arm. "You have to. It's time."

Cat sucked in a deep breath. She had no choice, she thought as she took Becca's hand.

"I'll go to the lobby and make some more calls. See what I can find out on my end," Cameron said, heading toward the door.

"I'll go with you." Kyle quickly followed.

"Thanks," Cat murmured as they walked out the door. She took Genie's hand along with Becca's, closed her eyes, and concentrated like she had countless times before when they were children. Focusing on the feel of their skin in hers, their warmth, the air flowing through her nostrils, and filling her lungs. She opened herself up, beyond the sounds in the room—the footsteps in the hall, the whir from traffic outside the windows—and instead listened with her other senses, the ones buried deep inside.

She visualized the wall in her mind—big and pliable —and pushed against it. It didn't budge. She tried again. Nothing happened but a small ache in her temples. She pushed harder, trying to break through the barrier she'd built, and the ache became a throb.

"I can't." She dropped her sisters' hands.

"You're fighting it," Becca said.

"Why would I do that?" Cat demanded and took a step back.

"Maybe you don't want to know what your husband is thinking and what secrets he's keeping from you." Becca's voice was sharp. Accusatory.

And all too true.

"Don't be ridiculous," Cat yelled. "If Tom is in trouble, I will do anything to help him. Anything."

Genie touched Becca on the arm. "Why don't you go check on Cameron and Kyle?"

Becca's eyes flared, then her mouth tightened and she stormed from the room.

"Don't need to be an empath to read her," Cat muttered.

Genie grinned. "Becca's always let it hang way out there." She sat on the sofa and patted the cushion next to her. "Tell me what's going on."

Cat sat and turned to face her. "I don't know, maybe Becca's right. Maybe I've always known Tom's been hiding something, and rather than face what he really thinks of me and our marriage, I've turned a blind eye."

"Do you think he's in danger?" Genie asked.

Cat stared into her sister's blue eyes that looked so much like her own and tried to answer truthfully. "I'm not sure."

"Okay, let's focus on what we do know. He told you he was here for a conference."

"Yes, he's been going to a lot more of them recently."

"Do you ever join him at these conferences?"

"No. He's never invited me." Cat's voice dropped as she realized how much the admission hurt.

Genie paused. "Have you ever had reason to doubt he wasn't where he said he was?"

"No. Never." Cat shook her head.

"Then chances are he's fine, but let's be sure and try again." She took Cat's hands in hers. "Close your eyes and think about Tom. The color of his eyes. His smile. The way he looks at you when he's happy. The touch of his lips on yours."

Cat felt herself smiling as the images moved through her head.

"Reach for him with your mind. Try to connect with him, to send him your love."

Cat's eyes opened. "Trees. I caught a glimpse of trees."

"Good. Anything else?"

Cat shook her head. "No."

"Any emotions? Fear?"

"No."

"It's a start. Keep practicing. Calm your breathing, center your feelings. Ground yourself."

"All right." Cat thought back to the exercises she did as a child. She'd once been a strong empath, easily able to read those around her. She could do this.

She held tight to Genie's hands and did as she said, digging deep, pushing against the walls surrounding her abilities. She pushed hard, refusing to give in to the fear and doubts circling her mind.

"I smell the woods." She smiled. "It smells nice."

"Good," Genie said. "What else?"

"Trees. Dirt. Shoes." Cat's eyes opened. "He's on foot in the woods. It feels like he's nowhere near San Francisco."

"Great," Genie said, smiling.

"Why would he be in a forest?" Cat wondered aloud.

There was a knock on the door. Genie rose to answer it, and Cameron walked in with Becca and Kyle. Cat stood.

"You're going to want to sit for this," Cameron said, but it was the look on Becca's face that had fear chasing through her.

Cat sat with Genie and Becca on either side of her, each taking her hand.

Cameron took a seat in the chair across from her. "As of this afternoon, Tom was okay."

"Okay." Cat waited for the other shoe to drop.

"Tom is not a pharmaceutical salesman. He is FBI and he's here on an assignment."

"FBI?" Cat repeated.

"What kind of assignment?" Genie asked.

"That's not possible," Cat said. "Why would he keep something like that from me?" She looked at Genie and then Becca. "Especially after everything he knows about us and our family. About the CTA."

"I'm guessing that was exactly why," Cameron said. "He didn't want any of us prying into what he's doing."

Becca pointed to the pistol still lying on the desk. "If he's on assignment, why did he leave his gun behind?"

"You said he was fine as of this afternoon. Why is that?" Cat asked.

"His partner, Sam Wagner, was tracking his progress into the California mountains. A couple of hours ago, Tom lost cell service. They aren't sure where he is."

5

Cat's heart lurched in her chest.

Genie turned to her, squeezing her hand. "We're going to try again. There's no holding back. If you want to find Tom, you're going to have to go all in. Are you willing to do that?"

Cat's eyes burned as she nodded. "Yes, I'm willing."

Genie smiled. "Good. Now let's try again. Close your eyes and take a deep breath."

Cat focused on her breathing, on relaxing, and going back to that place where the images would come.

"Think of Tom's voice in the morning, the smell of his cologne mingled with the steam from a hot shower," Genie said softly.

Cat felt her mind opening, gears clicking into place. An avalanche of emotions, images, and voices fell over her, and she gasped for air. "I can't breathe."

"Let them in slowly. One impression at a time," Becca said. "You can do this. You are in control."

"Pull in another deep breath and hold it. Focus on my voice," Genie added. "One... Two... Three... Okay, now let it out, slowly. Good, now do it again. Breathe in...and out."

Cat did as her sister asked, holding her breath, pushing out the voices, the images, the fear, and then slowly pulled in a new breath and let them back in. One at a time, and only those that pertained to Tom. She thought about the taste of his lips, the warmth of his touch. The way his hair fell over his forehead and glistened in the sunlight. The way his eyes crinkled when he smiled. The deep rumble of his laugh.

Suddenly, she felt a sharp object push into the middle of her back. Tension pulled across her shoulders as her hands were bound behind her.

"Move!"

The command shot through her mind. A hard shove on her shoulder caused her to stumble over a tree root sticking up from the path.

Her eyes shot open. "Oh my God! Tom's in trouble."

"What did you see?" Genie asked.

"He's in the woods. Someone has a gun to his back. His hands are bound behind him, and they're pushing him."

"They're? How many?" Becca asked.

"I don't know. I think two men," she said helplessly.

"That's good. Did you see anything that could help us locate him?" Genie asked.

"No. I didn't see anything other than trees. It's more

that I felt everything." She stood and started to pace. "He's in the mountains somewhere. How in the world are we going to find him?"

"We know he rented a Range Rover," Kyle said, ending his call. "And according to the vehicle's GPS, he is about five hours north of here."

Cat jumped to her feet. "Then let's go. You have a helicopter, don't you?"

"I do." Kyle picked up Tom's gun and tucked it in his waistband under his jacket. Before they could gather their things, there was another knock at the door. Cameron pulled his gun and stood behind the door as Kyle opened it.

"Sam," Cat greeted as she spied the man in the doorway carrying an armload of dresses wrapped in plastic.

"Mrs. Phillips." Sam looked at Cat from the doorway, then he nodded at Kyle. "I'm Special Agent Sam Wagner from the FBI's New York field office. Tom and I have been here for the last week working a case. Is Mr. Cameron here?"

Kyle nodded and opened the door further to allow Sam to enter, then held out his hand. "Kyle Montgomery."

Cameron stepped from behind the door and extended his hand. "Josh Cameron, head of the CTA. Thank you for coming."

"Good to meet you," Sam said with a nod.

"You mean you weren't here for a pharmaceutical conference?" Becca asked dryly.

"No, ma'am. I'm sorry. We weren't." He looked a little confused as his gaze swung from Becca to Cat to Genie.

"Triplets," Kyle said with a grin. He nodded toward the dresses. "What are those?"

"Delivery for the woman Tom was working with. We think her husband may have discovered she was talking to us. She disappeared this morning before Tom was supposed to meet with her."

"How do you know she didn't leave on her own?" Genie asked.

"We're not sure, except she left before her dresses were delivered. I thought if you were going up to her estate you could take these with you. They might give you a way in."

"Good thinking," Genie said, taking the dresses from him.

"That's what I planned when the boss called and said to read you in on the case. I must say, I was surprised. This entire op has been very hush-hush."

"We appreciate you working with us," Cameron said.

"Who is this woman Tom's been talking with?" Cat asked, not liking the edge to her voice. But this man had been lying to her for a solid year. He owed her the truth.

"Her name is Anita Bodega." Sam hesitated as he looked at the women, his unease clear.

"Your boss assured me we've been cleared to be

read in on what you have so far. All of us," Cameron reiterated.

Sam nodded. "Tom was concerned Mrs. Bodega's husband discovered she'd been talking to him and took her. She was supposed to give us intel that could do significant damage to his organization. After we realized she was gone, Tom went after her."

"Are you talking about Carlos Bodega? The notorious Cartel head from South America?" Kyle's voice was filled with surprise.

Sam nodded. "The one and only."

"But how?" Kyle asked.

"His wife contacted us a few weeks ago. We've been working hard to gain her trust. She asked us to find a way to protect her sisters. Tom worked all night arranging for the girls to be transferred to a safe house, but when he arrived at Mrs. Bodega's room this morning to get the intel she'd promised, she was gone."

"Gone?" Kyle asked.

"Taken. There were signs of a struggle, and she left without picking up her delivery this morning." He pointed to the dresses.

Becca grabbed the dresses. "Then we'll have to deliver them ourselves."

"Sam and I will head over to the local FBI office and make sure we're not crashing anyone's party," Cameron said. "Fly up there, but don't do anything until you get the go-ahead from me."

"Make it quick," Becca said as they all left the room. "This whole op sounds hokey to me. How do you even know the wife had something to give you? She could have just wanted her sisters protected and was playing you all along."

Sam shrugged. "Tom trusted her."

"Excuse me if I don't put a lot of faith in Tom's judgment right now," Becca said as they walked out of the elevator and through the lobby.

Cat had to admit, for once she agreed with Becca.

They hailed a taxi outside the hotel and headed for the airport and Kyle's helicopter. It took half an hour to get there, and another two hours to get near the area where the Range Rover was parked. When Cameron finally called, Kyle put him through to all their headsets.

"We've got a problem," Cameron said.

"We always have a problem," Becca replied. "What is it this time?"

"Apparently the San Francisco field office wasn't aware Tom was here working the case. According to Sam, he and Tom were worried about Carlos learning about his wife, so only a handful of people even know about the op."

"So that means he's on his own," Genie said.

"Yep. No one was watching his back," Cameron said, sending a chill down Cat's spine.

"What about Sam?" she asked.

"He was doing the best he could with limited resources. It's the Bodega estate you're flying toward. If you land there, chances are none of you will be coming back out. The FBI is ordering us to stand down. They don't want an international incident."

"What are we supposed to do about Tom? Leave him?" Cat asked, unable to believe what she was hearing.

"If we can prove Carlos has him, then they'll go in," Cameron said.

"In other words, they're not going to storm the house of an international Cartel head just because his wife is worried that her husband hasn't called home," Kyle said.

"Exactly." Cameron's all-business voice echoing through the speaker set Cat's teeth on edge.

"We're not coming back without him," Becca barked into the headset. Cat could have kissed her.

"How about we land outside the perimeter of the estate and go in on foot and see what we can find," Kyle offered.

"Isn't that what Tom did?" Genie asked.

Kyle gave her a wink. "Yep, but we're going in ready for trouble."

6

Tom woke to a bucket of ice water hitting his face. His eyes flew open as he quickly sat up. Pain shot through the back of his head. He winced and tried to reach for his head, but his right wrist was chained to the wall behind the cot he was lying on.

"Good, you're awake," a heavily accented voice said.

Carlos. "Where am I?" Tom asked.

"You're a guest at my house."

Tom looked around the dim basement room. There were no windows in the concrete walls, and the only light came from a single bulb hanging from the ceiling. Meager furnishings consisted of the cot and a single chair sitting over a large drain in the floor. Tom tried not to look at the drain or think about why it was there. The only way out appeared to be an iron circular staircase in the corner. "I think there's been some kind of mistake. I've never seen you before."

"What were you doing walking around my property?" Carlos asked.

Two men in fatigues stood behind him in the gloom, one still holding the bucket, the other holding an AR-15 pointed straight at him.

"I wasn't aware this place was even here. I just pulled off the side of the road to stretch my legs. You know how it is when nature calls." He had to get out of there.

"Is this the man you saw talking to Anita in the hotel?" Carlos asked.

The guard holding the bucket stepped out of the shadows. Slicked-back hair and dark eyes that narrowed as he looked down at him, Tom recognized the man from the bar. His heart sank.

The guard nodded. "Si, Señor."

Carlos stepped closer. "I understand my Anita is a beautiful woman. That men find her desirable, but to think you could share more than a drink with her, to follow her home, was a huge mistake."

"I don't know what you're talking about." Tom's palms were slick with sweat.

Carlos nodded and the guard stepped forward, threw down the bucket, and swung his fist, his knuckles connecting with Tom's nose. A cracking sound filled his head as pain exploded in his face. Blood spewed from his nostrils and pinpricks of light filled his vision. He gasped a breath, his head dropping back as he tried to staunch the flow of blood running down his face.

Carlos held up the picture of Anita Tom had been carrying in his pocket. "You want to try that again?"

Tom shrugged and smiled. "What can I say? She's a beautiful woman."

Carlos nodded again. The man stepped forward and hit him, again and again, until the room wavered. Tom fell back on the cot, buried his face in the rough fabric, and hunched his shoulders around his head. He didn't move and hoped they would leave. He didn't know how long he'd been down there in that room but prayed it had been long enough Sam was coming for him. As long as Carlos didn't know he was FBI, he might have a chance.

He thought of Cat. How long would she wait before calling someone? A week? A month? Would she even care that he was gone? When had they stopped talking to one another? Stopped pretending everything was okay? Sam would come. He clung to that belief as the guard continued to pummel him around his back and ribs. The room started to spin, and nausea turned his stomach.

He'd make it out of there and back to his family—to Mark and Annie.

To *Cat*.

He had to.

7

"I'm not leaving Tom behind," Cat said through the headset. She didn't know why, but she had to find him. Panic rose in her chest, and she was finding it hard to breathe.

"I'm sorry, but we can't defy orders." Cameron's voice was apologetic.

"We go off book all the time," Becca cried. "It's kind of what we do."

"Not this time," Cameron said. "This is the FBI's op."

"I don't work for the FBI," Cat said. "I'm a wife who's worried about her husband, and I don't take orders—not from him, and certainly not from the FBI. I'm going to find Tom. He's in trouble. I know it."

Genie took her hand and squeezed. "I know you're worried, but we can't let you walk in there alone."

"Why not? I'll be going in as a wife. Not an agent."

"It could work," Kyle said through the headpiece. "If

Tom's cover hasn't been blown. He's just a guy who was walking in the woods."

"But if you're wrong, you're flying into a trap," Cameron insisted.

"It's a chance we're willing to take," Kyle said with a grin. "We'll at least check out the Range Rover. Deliver the dresses. See what we can find out from Mrs. Bodega."

"Yes, we'll keep to the plan and say we're from the dress shop," Genie said.

"All right," Cameron relented. "From the satellite images around the location of the vehicle, there is a huge compound deep in the woods. I'm sending the location to your satellite devices."

"Thanks, Cameron. I appreciate it," Cat said.

"Just stay safe, and don't do anything that will make me regret this."

"In other words, keep a low profile," Genie said.

"We'll be in and out before anyone even knows what's happening," Becca assured him.

"I'll hold you to that," Cameron said and ended the call.

"Kyle, you drop us at the Range Rover. We'll take the car and drive up to the gates, here," Genie pointed to the gates on the satellite. "We'll say Mrs. Bodega left the city before our shop could deliver the dresses to her. She is such a valued customer, we wanted to send the dresses in person."

"Us?" Cat asked.

"Of course, all three of us," Genie said with a grin. "We're not letting you go in there alone."

Cat reached for her arm and squeezed it. "Thanks, Genie."

"All right," Kyle said. "I'll wait for you up the hill. Call if you need me, and I'll be right there."

Genie picked up the SAT phone. "We're counting on it."

"There's the Range Rover." Becca pointed at the car below them.

Kyle dropped the helicopter on the road next to the vehicle. The sisters jumped out, taking the dresses and the SAT phone with them, then they watched the helicopter fly out of sight.

"Let's go," Genie said, and they climbed into the Range Rover. Cat found the keys under the mat. Luckily, Tom stuck to his habits. Cat started the vehicle and drove down the hill, then turned into the long drive leading to the gates and the Bodega estate.

"Look at this place," Becca said as they drove down the paved road surrounded on either side with chain-link fence topped with razor wire.

"What do you think the chances are Mrs. Bodega gave the dress shop her actual address?" Cat asked.

"Slim to none," Genie answered.

"Let's hope the guards don't know that," Becca grumbled as a large gate with four armed guards positioned at strategic points came into view.

Cat rolled down her window as she stopped in front of the gate next to the guard booth. One of the guards stepped toward her. "Good afternoon. I'm here to see Mrs. Bodega," she said with a wide smile.

He frowned. "Is she expecting you?"

"I'm not sure." Cat grimaced and tilted her head with a slight please-help-me smile. "I'm afraid Mrs. Bodega left before I could deliver her dresses to her."

Becca held up the designer bag of dresses from the passenger seat.

"I know Mrs. Bodega has an event coming up and she needs these, so I took a chance and brought them to her myself." She leaned toward him and said conspiratorially, "She's my best client. I want to keep her happy. Can you give her a call and check for me? I'm sure she'll want to see us."

"Why don't you leave the bag here with me? I'll make sure she get's it," the guard offered.

Cat noticed a camera attached to the wall of the booth turn toward her. "I'm afraid she has to try the dresses on. What if they don't fit? Then she'd have to come all the way back to the city to get them altered. That's why I brought my best seamstress with me." She pointed to Becca.

"All right, let me call the house and check," he said, walking back into the booth.

"Thank you so much," Cat said as he made the call. After a moment, he hung up the phone and nodded to the guard standing on the other side of the gate. The man opened it and they drove through.

"All right," Genie said. "One hurdle crossed." She

held up the SAT phone and pushed the call button. "We're going in."

"Copy that," Kyle answered.

They proceeded down the road, the continuous barricade of wire hemming them in. "That's not suspicious at all," Becca said. "Who is this guy?"

"Apparently someone who values his privacy."

Cat parked the car in front of an impressive Spanish mansion made from stucco and Spanish tiles. The dark wooden rough-hewn front door, decorated with an iron door pull and hinges, was massive. "Wow," she said. "Just a little intimidating."

All three got out of the car and walked toward the house, Becca carrying the dresses slung over her arm. The door opened and an older housekeeper nodded, gesturing for them to come in. She led them into a large office off the foyer where a man who looked to be in his early forties sat behind a beautiful mahogany desk. Behind him, French doors were open to a walled-in courtyard complete with a large flowing fountain.

"Who are you?" Annoyance filled his face as he looked up.

Cat pulled a stack of receipts clipped together off the dresses and handed them to him, sticking the paper clip in her pocket. "We're from Daisy's Designer Dresses in San Francisco. Mrs. Bodega left before we could make the delivery to the hotel this morning. She said she has several events lined up and it's important we get her fitted for these dresses right away. Is she home?"

The man stared at her for a long moment, his fingers playing with the receipts. "I'm sorry you came all this way to deliver my wife's dresses, but she's not here. She's still in the city."

"What? In the city? They told me at the hotel she'd already checked out and left for home." Cat's eyes widened with incredulity.

His annoyance turned to concern. "This is why I allowed you to come in. I need to know where my wife is. I haven't been able to get in touch with her, and I'm very worried. When you showed up, claiming to have spoken to her with a car full of dresses, well, you can understand why I thought we should speak."

Cat blinked. She turned to Genie and Becca who just shrugged. "Of course. I don't know how this could have happened."

"I'm afraid we're just as confused as you are," Genie added.

He stood. "Well, Ms.?"

"Daisy," Cat said, gesturing toward the receipts. "From Daisy's Dresses."

He stared at her for a long moment, shaking his head. "I would like to believe you, but you haven't uttered a truthful word since you arrived. Leave the dresses and get out of my house." He nodded to a man who appeared in the doorway with slicked-back black hair and eyes so dark, fear fluttered in Cat's stomach.

Cat frowned. "I'm sorry? I don't understand."

"Let's just say I'm a very important man with many enemies. So, when my wife goes to the city for one of her shopping excursions, I always have people keep an eye on her. For her safety, of course."

"Of course," she muttered. *Yeah, right. More likely your wife is your prisoner.*

"My people have told me you were also at the hotel this morning looking for your husband. Is that not true?"

Cat's eyes drifted closed as she sighed. "Yes, it's true," she admitted, her mind quickly spinning a new tactic.

"So, once again, tell me why you think your husband would be here?" Mr. Bodega asked.

"Your wife was the last person he spoke to," Cat said, improvising. "He's disappeared and I was hoping he might have told her where he was planning to go. The police are absolutely no help. They think he just ran off to blow off some steam or something and not to worry. They said he'll show up. Can you believe that?"

He didn't say anything, just studied her with a direct gaze that made her want to avert her eyes. She shook her head, instead. "I must admit, I thought he might be having an affair with your wife." *Where did that come from?* She knew better. She trusted Tom. And yet, what did she even know about him? He'd been lying to her for years, and she hadn't had a clue. "But that was just my fear talking. I know he'd never do that," she said.

"You don't work for the dress shop, do you?" Carlos asked.

"No," Cat admitted, deciding a little honesty would

probably be best. "The dresses were delivered to the hotel this morning after Mrs. Bodega left."

"She was already gone, as was your husband." His cold gaze met hers. "So you thought you'd look for him here?"

She took a deep breath and shrugged. "I had no other clues. I didn't think he was here; I hoped your wife would know where he might be. I even dragged my sisters with me just in case." She offered a self-deprecating smile.

He laughed. "So you consider yourself an amateur sleuth? Come on, tell the truth. You believe your husband and my wife ran off together, and you're hoping I'll help you find them." He laughed, the sound reverberating around the room. "Anita would never do that; she knows better." The look in his eyes sent a shiver down her spine.

"Then where are they?" Cat heard the fear in her voice. This man had a way of twisting and turning everything she said.

He stood and walked around his desk. "I don't know, but I can assure you I will find out. Tony will escort you back to your car. Leave your number with him and I'll contact you as soon as my people find out anything."

She let out a deep sigh and forced a wide smile as she shook his hand. "Thank you, Mr. Bodega. I can't tell you how much better that makes me feel."

The pure evil emitting from his touch made her

blood run cold. He smiled, his eyes lighting with appreciation. "Sisters, huh?"

"Yes, triplets," she squeaked and pulled her hand back.

"I can see that." The desire filling his face, his suggestive body language, and the sick feeling turning in her stomach caused by his touch, had bile rising up her throat.

"I will be in touch. Thank you for bringing my wife's dresses."

She turned and followed Tony out of the office. Their heels clicked on the Spanish tiles as she and her sisters walked through the large entryway. Before they reached the massive wood and iron door, she heard something. She paused, her eyes catching Becca's as a tickle moved in the back of her mind.

A voice. A woman's voice.

Help me.

She called to Tony. "Excuse me. I'm sorry to bother you. It's such a long drive back to the city. Do you mind if I use your restroom?"

"Me, too," Becca said with a smile.

He hesitated for a moment and looked at Genie, eyebrows raised.

"Oh, I'm good," she said.

He nodded and gestured toward a side hall. Cat gave him a grateful smile before she and Becca hurried the way he pointed.

"So, tell me about the house, it's beautiful." She heard Genie making small talk with Tony while she and Becca entered the bathroom. The way Tony had been staring at them, Genie should be able to keep his attention for a while. Whether Tom was here or not, someone in this house needed help.

"I heard a woman say *help me*," she whispered to Becca.

Becca grinned and peeked out the bathroom door. "Good, your abilities are coming back. Reach for her with your mind. Can you tell where she is?"

Cat shook her head. "No, the voice was faint."

"Same for me," Becca said. "Let's check the rooms on this hall. I'll take the ones on the right; you take the left. Be quick…and careful."

Cat nodded and followed her sister out of the bathroom. She reached for Tom with her mind. *Where was he? He has to be there.* She started opening doors, peeking into the rooms. Every one of them was empty and there was no one in sight. She was drawn to the last door at the end of the hall. She glanced behind her as she hurried toward it but saw no one.

She opened the door, but instead of another bedroom she saw a circular iron staircase leading down into the darkness.

"Hello," she whispered.

Something moved below. She entered the stairwell, softly shut the door behind her, and was enveloped in darkness. She took out her phone, turned on the flashlight, and inhaled a deep breath for courage as she carefully descended the stairs.

8

Footsteps descended the stairs. Tom cracked open his eyes. He couldn't believe what he saw in the dim light. He must be dreaming. He closed his eyes again.

"Tom!"

He looked at her from his narrow cot. "Cat?"

She rushed to his side. "Oh my God. Look at you."

"What are you doing here?" He blinked his eyes in disbelief. He had to be imagining things. This couldn't be possible.

Her fingers lightly grazed his face. He could only imagine what he looked like. Worry swam in her eyes. *Was she really here?*

Fear shot through him and he sat up. Pain and dizziness swam through his head, making his stomach turn. "You can't be here."

"I'm rescuing you." Alarm played heavy across her face. "But we don't have a lot of time, so you need to get up."

He didn't want to think about what Carlos would do to her if he discovered her there. "But how did you find me?" No one knew where he was.

"Does that matter? We have to go." She pulled on him.

He held up his right hand. He was chained to the bed. "You have to leave me. Hurry. Go get help."

"I am the help, and I'm not leaving you." She picked up the lock attached to the shackles on his wrist and pulled the paper clip out of her pocket and quickly used it to pick the lock.

This wasn't possible. They must have drugged him, and he was hallucinating.

"I've already been gone too long." She grabbed his hand and pulled.

"How did you know how to do that?" He teetered on his feet and leaned against her. His ribs were bruised, his head spinning. She helped him up the stairs, one agonizingly slow step at a time.

"Becca and Genie are in the foyer."

Becca and Genie? Her sisters. Of course.

They reached the landing at the top of the stairs. "We have your car out front. Is there any way you get to it on your own?" She cracked open the door and peered into the hall.

"I'm not sure," he admitted. He wavered slightly and held her tighter. She eased him into the hall and shut the door behind them.

The door across from them opened and Becca gestured her forward. "This way."

They followed her into a sitting room with French doors leading onto the front porch that ran the length of the house. Cat pointed to his Range Rover. "I'll meet you at the car," she whispered, then left him leaning against the wall as she and Becca slipped out the door back into the hall.

He stumbled across the room, clutching the sofa as he moved toward the French doors, and eased out of the house. He saw his car parked a mere fifty feet away. He made his way across the covered walkway, avoiding the needle-like thorns of the bougainvillea bushes that encircled the porch's columns.

Suddenly three men in fatigues and carrying AR-15s appeared out of nowhere. "Look what we have here," the one in front said, a wide smile on his sun-bronzed face.

"Damn," Tom muttered under his breath. His car was so close, he could practically touch it, but there was no way he'd be able to get there. He could barely even move.

"Let's go." The guards gestured him forward with their guns.

He had no choice. He was outgunned and outnumbered. He walked toward the front door, reaching it just as it opened and Cat and her sisters walked out. They all stopped. Cat's eyes widened with fear.

He shrugged. *Sorry, babe.*

Carlos appeared behind them, and his heart tightened in his chest. "Sorry to disrupt your plans, ladies, but I've decided I'd like you all to be my guests for dinner."

He turned to his guards. "Take them to their accommodations in the West wing and be sure to bring me any identification these beautiful women might have on their persons. I'm very curious to learn who they really are."

The guard shoved Tom forward. He tripped but regained his balance before falling. His stomach dropped as he looked at Cat and her sisters. They'd be lucky if any of them made it out alive. The guard pushed him back down the hall toward the same room he'd been in earlier. Back to the darkness. Only this time the torture would be wondering what that animal and his men were doing to his wife and her sisters.

The brutish guard opened the door. Tom stepped onto the staircase's landing, then felt a shove against his back. He grabbed hold of the iron rail to keep from falling down the stairs. Pain shot through his middle as he twisted his bruised ribs. He gritted his teeth as sweat broke out on his forehead.

"Watch it," he heard Cat bark and cringed, praying the guards wouldn't touch her.

He heard laughter, then the door slammed shut. Cat put her arm around his shoulders to keep him steady as they descended the stairs. Thankfully, the light had been left on. For now.

Tom made his way back to the cot and sat down, not moving for a moment while he waited for the pain to subside. He felt the cot shift next to him and turned toward Cat, defeat and sorrow in his gut. "Why are you here? Do you know how much trouble we're in?"

Her gaze moved over his face. She reached out to touch his swollen eye and bloodied nose. "How about you explain to me exactly what you're doing here?"

He hesitated for a brief second, debating what to tell her. Wondering how much she already knew about what he did for a living. "I'm sorry."

"For what? That you lied about what you were doing in San Francisco? Or that you followed a woman into the mountains, putting us both in grave danger?"

He didn't respond. Didn't know what to say.

"Or about the fact that our entire marriage has been built on a huge lie."

"Cat…"

"Or maybe the truth is you're here because you're involved with another woman." Her eyes held his for a long moment.

"Is that what you think?"

"Did you sleep with her?" she asked, jumping to her feet.

"Of course not," he said quickly, even as he thought of Anita's brilliant green eyes and the soft touch of her hand on his.

Pain filled Cat's face before her eyes narrowed with anger. "Maybe not, but you want to."

"I have always been faithful to you," he said, knowing it wasn't nearly enough.

"Physically, maybe. But you haven't been there. Not for a long time. You know it's true, now own it."

He didn't know what to say; she was right. "I never touched Anita."

"But you're attracted to her."

"She's a beautiful woman. But I wouldn't have acted on that attraction. You are my wife, and yes, we're having problems, big problems, but that doesn't mean I've been unfaithful."

"So you might be a liar, but you're not a cheater?"

The sharp words stung, especially since they were true.

"I'm sorry," he said again.

"I'm pretty sure that's not good enough anymore."

His heart sunk. "I know I blew it. I don't deserve you, and I haven't appreciated you or our family. Please, just give me a chance to make it up to you."

"You're assuming we're going to get out of this," she said, gesturing her arms wide.

"We will." He reached for her. "I have faith."

She stared at his outstretched hand before taking it and sitting back beside him on the cot. After a moment, she said, "I can hear you singing that song in my head. Do you remember? You used to sing it all the time."

He smiled slightly. "That seems like a long time ago."

"Too long."

He leaned close, his head next to hers. "I want to tell you everything, but I'm pretty sure the reason we're in the same room right now is because we're being watched."

"Then tell this man where his wife is. That's all he wants to know," Cat said.

Confusion swam through him. "What are you talking about?"

She reached for his hand and squeezed. "He's looking for her too. She disappeared from the hotel this morning."

Questions swam through Tom's mind. Was there a chance Carlos didn't know he was FBI? Did Anita use them as a way to escape from her marriage? Maybe she never had any intention of helping him; maybe she just wanted him to protect her sisters so she could disappear. If that was the case, he'd walked into a trap. Once Carlos discovered Sarah and Savannah were gone, he'd do anything to find out where they went. *Anything*.

"I swear to you, I don't know where his wife is. I met her at the hotel yesterday. Got the feeling she was in trouble. The girl at the desk said she left in a black SUV this morning, so I followed. That's all."

"She didn't. She's not here," Cat said.

"I swear to you, I thought she was."

She rested her head on his shoulder. "I sure hope he believes you."

He breathed deep her sweet scent. It had been a long time since he'd been this close to her. "Me, too."

After a moment, she stood. "Come on, let's go."

He looked up in surprise. "Go where?"

"We're getting out of here." She took his hand and helped him up the stairs.

"You know he's watching us," he whispered.

"More than likely." She put her ear to the door, then turned to him. "Step back." They moved to the far side of the stairwell's landing just as the door swung open and Becca stuck her head inside.

"Ready?" She handed Cat an AR-15.

"Ready." Cat smiled and allowed Tom to take the gun from her as they followed Becca out the door. Three of Carlos' guards were on the ground, their guns slung over Becca and Genie's shoulders.

He stared at his wife of ten years and realized he didn't have a clue who she was, nor what she was capable of.

"What about Anita?" he asked. "He was lying to you. She is here. I'm certain of it. I followed the SUV she was in."

Cat turned to him, a look of disbelief on her face. "So what if she is? We can't stay."

"I've been trying to turn her. To get intel on her husband. It's my fault she's in trouble. You don't know what he will do to her. The man is an animal."

"Not our problem," Genie said, rushing down the hall toward the front door. "All that matters right now is that we get out of here."

Maybe not *their* problem, but Anita definitely was his. He hadn't even managed to get proof she was here at the estate. He needed something to take to the FBI, or he didn't have a chance in hell of getting a team together to rescue her. His ribs ached as he rushed to follow Cat. The sad truth was, he wasn't in any condition to do anything about it. He'd failed.

9

CAT TURNED to Tom who had stopped in the middle of the foyer. She could feel his hesitation, his frustration. "Tom, come on," she insisted.

"We can't leave without Anita. Carlos will kill her."

"He'll kill us. Think about Mark and Annie. Think about your family."

They heard footsteps coming down the hall. Fast.

"Cat, come on," Genie called. Becca was already running toward the Range Rover. Cat grabbed Tom's hand and pulled. "You can't help her if you're dead."

He relented and they ran out the door and toward the car.

Becca climbed in the driver's seat and started the engine. Genie close behind, with Cat and Tom hurrying toward them. They dove into the back seat as Becca got the car rolling. Once they were inside, she tore up the drive.

Cat didn't need to be a mind reader to see the

torment Tom was in. "There was nothing we could have done," she told him and touched his arm. "The estate is huge. She could be anywhere."

"And yet you found me." Fire burned in his eyes. "You still haven't told me how."

Is she that important to you? Cat swallowed the words before she could ask.

Becca swung the Range Rover to the left, following the drive down around the back of the house instead of going up the road to the gates and the main road. And Kyle.

"Where are you going?" Genie yelled, grabbing the door pull to keep from being thrown out of her seat.

"To find this Anita," Becca yelled.

Tom leaned forward. "Thank you."

"Don't thank me. I'm not doing it for you; I'm doing it for her."

"Becca, you're going to get us all killed," Genie cried.

Becca grinned. "Ye of little faith. We've been in bigger jams than this and survived."

"Maybe, but look at this place!" Genie said. "You know Carlos has a lot more guards than the three we took care of, and by now, he knows we're gone. Besides, don't you remember our promise to Cameron?"

"Don't worry. We got this." Becca stepped on the gas.

"How do you know where she is?" Tom asked as

they continued past the house and deeper into the forest.

"I can hear her," Becca said. "Faintly, but it's getting stronger."

"You what?" Tom turned to Cat, his eyebrows raised.

"I did too," Cat admitted. "Once. Faintly. When we were in the house. Before I found you." She ignored the look on Tom's face, not sure if it was anger, disgust, or fear. All of which weren't good and instead focused on that little scratching noise in her mind. It was growing louder.

Becca stopped in front of a small stucco building with iron bars on the windows.

"It looks like a jail," Cat said, trying to squelch her nervousness.

"Let's try not to think about what Carlos uses this place for," Genie said as they climbed out of the Rover.

"Okay, Genie and Cat, you go around back," Becca ordered. "Make sure we aren't surprised. Tom, you're with me. Can you handle it?"

Tom's brows shot up, and he looked like he was about to argue but changed his mind. Smart man. This might be Tom's case, but it was Becca's mission, all the way.

Cat and Genie ran around the back of the building. There were no windows or doors on this side, and the trees grew right up next to the house. There was no one here. They were about to circle around when Cat stopped.

"Wait," she said and pointed to what looked like a small surveillance camera pointed right at them.

Genie picked up a rock and struck the camera on her first try.

"Good job," Cat said with a grin.

"I was on the softball team in high school."

"I bet you were great. I would have been right there in the stands cheering for you."

"Not on the field with me?" Genie asked.

"No, I was more of the drama club type."

"Wish I could have seen that."

Their father had separated them after their mother died, changing their names and sending them to different boarding schools with instructions never to get in touch with one another. They grew up alone. Having lost their parents and each other in the blink of an eye. All to keep them safe. Cat was still recovering from the loss.

"I was pretty good," Genie said, pulling her out of her thoughts. "I'll come by sometime and show Mark and Annie a few tricks."

"We'd like that."

Genie put her arm around Cat's shoulders. "Come on, let's see how many more cameras we can find."

They slipped into the woods skirting the drive, looking for cameras and taking them out, one by one. They found six and were halfway back up the road when they heard the roar of Jeep engines.

"Run!" Cat yelled.

10

Tom followed Becca to the front door of the small house.

"Stand back," he said as he got ready to kick the door open.

She looked at him with raised brows, the doubt clear on her face. As he started to swing his leg, pain arced through his middle. He stopped, mid-swing, and grabbed his ribs. "Damn. I hope they're not broken."

"My turn." She stepped forward and planted her foot square against the door. It cracked and splintered. She swung back and kicked it again, and this time the door flew open. She turned to Tom and grinned, giving him a told-you-so look.

Tom shook his head and smiled; he'd been bested. He lifted the AR-15 and followed her through the door.

Anita was sitting in a chair against the wall, wrists tied to the arms, eyes wide as she saw him.

"Tom. Thank God you're here."

"Are you okay?" He scanned the room and saw a camera in the corner pointed at the door. He aimed the rifle and shot out the camera. The loud report filled the room, making Anita wince.

"Yes, I'm fine," she said, looking relieved as he hurried toward her.

Becca's eyebrows raised as she watched them. "Oh, brother," she muttered.

"Becca, can you check for any other cameras?"

He pulled at the ropes tying Anita's arms to the chair. "Do you have anything in this cabin that can cut these?"

"No," she said, biting her lip.

"Here." Becca threw him an all-purpose knife. Good quality, military-grade. He gave her a look of surprise. She shrugged. "I got it off one of the guards."

He cut the ropes, then helped Anita up, took her arm, and led her toward the door. She'd been sitting a long while and had trouble moving. "Do you have the information we need on Carlos' organization?"

"It's in my suite in the main house. We'll never be able to get it now. Not as long as Carlos is there."

"We have to go," Becca said as the whine of loud engines racing toward them filled the air.

They hurried toward the Range Rover, but four Jeeps arrived before they could get into the car. They ran back inside, where Tom hovered in the doorway of the bungalow.

"Where's Cat and Genie?" He scoured the area looking for any sign of his wife.

"Hopefully, still around back," Becca said under her breath.

"Come out with your hands up and we'll let you live," a heavily accented voice yelled. There were eight men out there, each with AR-15s pointed their way.

"Will they shoot at you?" Tom asked Anita.

She shrugged. "I don't know. Carlos thinks we were having an affair. He doesn't know about everything else."

"That's good. I hope."

"What are we going to do?" she asked.

"We're going to walk out of here, take their guns, flatten their tires, and be on our way," Becca said like it was the obvious move and no big deal.

"How are we going to manage that?" Tom asked. "There are eight of them out there, and we only have two guns."

"Yep, but they've messed with the wrong sisters."

He stared in disbelief as Genie and Cat crept up behind two of the guards lingering at the back of the group. Cat hit the one closest to her on the back of the head with a rock. He crumpled at her feet. She quickly took his gun. The guard closest to Genie turned at the sound of the blow. Genie shoved her gun into his chest and said something to him. He froze. She took his gun and handed it to Cat.

"Does she even know how to shoot that thing?" Tom asked.

Becca looked at him like he was an idiot. "Do you not know anything about your wife?"

Cat took the guard's knife off his hip, opened it, and stabbed one of the Jeep's tires, then quickly approached another guard and took him hostage, holding the knife to his neck. Suddenly there were only five and their odds were looking better.

"Stop and drop your guns or we will kill them," Genie yelled to the other guards, who had been busy moving toward the house. They turned back in surprise as she and Cat pushed their two hostages toward the bungalow.

"Maybe we'll just kill you instead," one of the men said, obviously the one in charge. He turned his gun and pointed it at Genie.

"Don't even think about it or your man's dead."

The sound of breaking glass filled the room as Becca shoved the barrel of her gun through the window.

The man pulled the trigger at the same time Becca did. Genie slipped behind the guard she was holding as a bullet tore through him. The man crumpled to the ground at her feet.

Becca's bullet tore into the guard that had fired. He fell.

Cat abandoned her hostage, dropping behind a Jeep, and started firing, pulling the trigger in quick succession. Between her and Becca firing through the window, the guards were collapsing as bullets littered the Jeeps and the bungalow.

Tom joined Becca at the window, firing on the guards that were attacking Cat and Genie. He watched his wife wield the lethal weapon, unable to comprehend what he was seeing. Cat's aim was dead-on. He didn't even know his wife knew how to shoot, but the way she handled that AR-15, she looked like a military sniper who'd been handling guns all her life.

The shooting stopped. No one moved.

"I suggest you drop your guns, or you're all dead," Becca called out the window. "We have you outnumbered."

The clatter of one gun falling to the ground was followed by two more.

"Okay, stand up and walk toward the bungalow with your hands in the air," Genie ordered from behind a Jeep.

Three men did as she said, walking forward with their hands up. Genie and Cat stood, guns pointed their way, and followed them into the bungalow.

"Any more rope?" Becca asked as she picked the pieces off the floor that had been used on Anita.

"I'll look in their vehicles," Tom said and hurried past Cat as she gestured one of the guards inside with her gun.

He found a bundle of rope, brought it inside, and tied up the trio of men. Once they were secure, he collected all the guns lying out front and put them in the Range Rover. "We better get going."

As they left the bungalow, Genie stabbed the tires of the remaining Jeeps and took all the radios. "That should slow them down."

Tom walked toward the driver's seat of the Range

Rover but before he could climb behind the wheel, Becca was standing next to him giving him that look. "Let me guess, you want to drive," he said.

"I think with your condition it's the right move. Don't you?"

He grinned. "I think I can handle a steering wheel."

"You never know what we're going to face. Get in the back." She jerked her head, all pretense of niceties over.

He did as she said, only because he didn't have time to fight, but the sooner he got away from Cat's sisters, the better.

"I can never repay you for rescuing me," Anita said as they raced up the drive toward the gate. "Carlos was enraged when I got back to the estate. I've never seen him so angry. I don't know what he would have done to me."

"Are you sure he doesn't know about our deal?" Tom asked.

"He knows my sisters have disappeared. Sarah's boyfriend called him when she didn't show up for their date. He knew I had something to do with it. But I didn't tell him."

"Any chance we can go back for your intel?" Tom asked.

"No way. Carlos has a lot more guards. We'll be lucky if we get out the gate and back to town before they catch up with us."

"We'll see about that," Genie said. She took a SAT phone out of her pocket and pushed the radio call button. "Hey, babe, you better get that engine running; we're on our way."

"Copy that."

"Who was that?" Tom asked.

"Kyle. You met him in Reno last year."

Tom winced, remembering a helicopter landing on his front lawn and taking his kids. "He CTA, too?"

"Yep," Genie said.

"As shocking as this day has been, I must admit, I'm impressed." His gaze met Cat's, but she didn't say anything as she glanced between him and Anita. He knew how this must look. And the worst part was he couldn't explain anything to her. Not yet.

"Duck down," Becca yelled.

Up ahead were four more Jeeps and a line of men standing in front of the gates, guns raised and pointed straight at them.

"We'll never make it through," Anita yelled.

Becca grinned and tightened her grip on the wheel. "Oh, yeah? Just watch."

11

Cat's grip tightened on the back of Genie's seat as she stared at the men and their guns in horror. How were they going to get through that line of guards?

Becca slammed the accelerator to the floor. "Hang on!"

"Becca!" Cat screamed, ducking her head as the men scattered.

"Stay down," Becca yelled as she scrunched in her seat and sped between the two Jeeps, plowing through the chain-link gate.

Cat threw herself across Tom's lap. His arm covered her as he protected her with his body. His love and fear for her rolling over and through her, so strong, so immediate, it brought tears to her eyes.

A hail of bullets hit the Range Rover, shattering the back window and peppering them with glass. Anita screamed and Cat felt a sting on her cheek as Becca barreled up the road.

"Anita, you're bleeding," Tom yelled, and suddenly all Cat could feel was Tom's fear for Anita. *His horror. His guilt.* "You've been shot!"

Cat looked up and gasped a quick alarmed breath. A bullet had torn through Anita's shoulder.

Tom pulled off his light-weight jacket, balled it up, and pressed it against her wound. "You're going to be okay. It looks like it went through. Just hold this against your shoulder."

Tears rolled down Anita's cheeks. "I can't believe they shot me."

"So much for marital bliss," Becca murmured and glanced at Cat through the rearview mirror, her eyebrows raised.

Cat glowered at her. Tom's concern for Anita was overwhelming. She sat up and stopped touching him, trying to tune his emotions out, to turn her abilities off even as she struggled to fight oncoming tears. Was her marriage over? Was it even worth saving?

The drive past the gates to the main road had to be at least half a mile, with several turns Becca took at dizzying speeds. As they reached the road, Becca turned left up the mountain without slowing.

"The town is the other way," Tom shouted and continued to look behind him for guards following. "Is there a hospital near here?" he asked Anita.

"I'm sure there is, and that is exactly where Carlos will expect us to go," Genie said. "But that's not where we're going."

"Anita needs to get to a hospital," he insisted as blood saturated his jacket.

"Almost there," Genie said into the phone.

When they turned the corner, a helicopter was sitting in the middle of the road, rotors spinning. Cat had never been so happy to see Kyle in her life. Even happier than when he pulled her off the roof of the casino last year in Reno. She needed to put some distance between her and Tom and his worry for Anita. She didn't want to *feel* him anymore.

Becca pulled the Range Rover off the road, and they all ran toward the helicopter. They climbed inside, Tom helping Anita up, their hair whipping around their heads.

"We have company!" Vehicles roared through the trees. Tom winced as he pulled himself up. Before they were all buckled in, Kyle was lifting off the ground.

Carlos' guards poured out of the vehicles, guns raised, and started firing.

"They're shooting at us!" Genie yelled.

Only a few bullets hit the helicopter as they soared higher in the sky, turning over the treetops and flying across the mountain range toward San Francisco.

Cat hoped the bullets that hit didn't cause any damage. She pulled on her headset and handed the extra to Tom. "Are we good?" she asked Kyle.

Kyle kept his gaze on the gauges for a long moment. Then said, "We're good."

Cat turned to Tom. "What's going to happen now?"

"When we get to San Francisco, we'll have to take Anita to a hospital, then check into the FBI field office and give them a report about what happened here today."

"Trust me, they're waiting for it," Kyle said through the headset. "Cameron's been calling me nonstop."

"Cameron?" Tom asked.

"Josh Cameron, head of the CTA."

Tom cringed. "So my secret undercover op that only a handful of people knew about is now known by the CTA?"

"And the San Francisco FBI field office," Kyle said.

"We know everything," Cat told him. "Your undercover days are going to be on hold for a while."

Tom's expression flattened for a moment as he processed her words, then he turned to Anita, his voice softening. The sound was a knife blade to Cat's heart. "If there is anything you can tell us about your husband's business, that would certainly help us explain this mess to the authorities and pull my butt out of the fire."

"What about my sisters? Are they safe?" Anita demanded.

"Are you kidding right now?" Becca yelled. "Do you have any idea what we just risked to rescue you? The trouble we're in?"

Anita's eyes widened and her lips trembled.

Tom took her hand, making Cat want to scream. How stupid could he be?

"Your sisters are safe," he assured her. "For now. Is

there anything you know that will help us protect them? And you?" Tom asked gently.

Anita stared at him for a long moment, obviously debating her options.

"Just tell him already," Cat said, her voice harsh. She was done with the two of them.

Anita bit her lip as her gaze met Cat's, then she turned back to Tom. "I have a book. Carlos calls it his little black book. It's a handwritten network of distributors across the United States. He doesn't trust computers so it's his only copy. I've hidden it in my rooms in the main house. But it won't be there for long. Once Carlos discovers it's gone, he'll tear the house apart to find it."

Tom wanted to go back. Cat could feel the need rolling through him. She couldn't believe it. The op was all that mattered to him. More than his own safety. *Or theirs.*

"You're both out of there; that's all that matters now," Genie said, her eyes meeting Cat's.

"Yes," Cat agreed. "Against extreme odds, we made it off that estate. That has to be a win."

Tom's eyes met hers and sent an ache through her chest. She wished she could be sure they still had a fighting chance. That their marriage was worth fighting for. Right now, she just didn't think they did.

12

Kyle landed the helicopter on the roof of San Francisco General Hospital where medical personnel were waiting for them to transfer Anita to the emergency room. While the medics got her settled on the gurney, Cat and the others got out to watch. With his hand on her arm, Tom took Cat aside to tell her he was staying until an agent from the San Francisco FBI field office could be assigned to protect her. "It will take a few hours. Will you be at the hotel when I get there? Or are you leaving with your sisters?"

He wasn't sure she'd stay, Cat realized. Truthfully, until that moment, she hadn't been sure herself.

"Yes. I think we have a lot to talk about." *Like our marriage and if it can be saved.*

He smiled slightly, then leaned in and gave her a quick sterile kiss. How many kisses had they shared like that over the years? *Too many.*

"Are you sure you're going to be okay?" Genie asked Cat as he followed Anita's gurney into the hospital.

Cat nodded. "I'll be fine. Tom and I just need some time alone to figure out what we're going to do. Changes have to be made. I don't want a marriage built on secrets and lies."

"I don't blame you."

"I've kept secrets too, but mine seem small compared to his."

Genie put her arm around her shoulders and pulled her close. "Give him a chance to explain."

Cat looked at her and smiled. "Thanks for always being there for me."

"Always. Kyle and I are only a short flight away if you need us. We're going back to the house to work with the people we've contacted from Tom Garrison's experiments. Cameron has received authorization under the CTA umbrella to start a new task force using agents with extraordinary abilities. We've found Emerich's facility where he's been holding others like us. Becca and Cameron are forming a rescue mission. We're trying to find as many as we can from the original ISO90 experiments and help them if they need it. Jayne and Marcie are back at the house now. We're training them on how to control their abilities. If you'd like to join us, we could use the help. I think it will be a lot of fun."

Cat loved the sound of that, and she really liked the idea of working with her sisters. "It sounds amazing and something I wouldn't mind being a part of. I'd like to make amends for all the damage Dad and Dr. Garrison have done to us and others. I'll call you tomorrow after Tom and I talk."

"Okay."

Becca walked toward her, arms out.

"Try and stay out of trouble," Cat said, walking into her hug.

"What fun is that?" Becca laughed. "Do yourself a favor and don't hold back. Turn your abilities on all the way. Trust yourself to be able to handle it."

"I will," Cat promised. She already had and could feel herself growing stronger by the moment. It felt good.

"Have a good night." She waved as her sisters got back into the helicopter and flew away. She almost wished she was going with them, but she couldn't. She had a marriage to save and a family to put back together.

In a daze, she walked in the hospital, caught the elevator to the main floor, then snapped out of it enough to hail a taxi. She realized her stomach hurt because she hadn't eaten all day and had the taxi stop in front of a Chinese restaurant a block from Tom's hotel. She ordered a late dinner to go, then brought it back to the room. She'd just finished setting it all out when Tom arrived.

"What's all this?" he asked as he came into the room.

"Dinner. I thought we should eat in the room so we can talk."

"Okay." He took a seat at the table and picked up

one of the square containers and opened it, spooning a healthy portion onto his plate. "Looks good. Smells even better. I'm famished."

"How's Anita?" she asked.

"Shaken, but she's going to be fine. She still can't believe Carlos ordered his men to shoot at her."

"I don't know why not. Did you get any more information out of her?"

"No. The book we need is back at the estate."

Cat grimaced.

"The FBI has been watching the satellite feeds of Carlos' compound since we left. Looks like Carlos is heading back to Columbia. He left an hour ago. His people are packing up the estate."

"If he's gone, then now would be a perfect time for us to go get this book," she said.

He looked at her eyebrows raised. "Us?"

"Yes, us. Why not?"

"For one thing, it's dangerous."

She grinned. "Yes."

"And for the other, you're not FBI."

"A problem that would only take a phone call to fix, you realize that, right?"

"Cat. You can't come." His eyes held hers.

She squared her shoulders. "Let me rephrase this for you. I'm not asking, and you're not going without me. You'd still be there locked in that basement, or worse, if it wasn't for me. You're not leaving me behind. Not anymore."

"What does that mean?"

"It means, we have a long drive. You're going to spend it telling me everything you've been hiding from me for the last ten years."

"I can't."

"You can. And you will." She felt his resistance roll off him like a tidal wave. "Do you want to stay married to me?" There she asked it. She hadn't planned on it, wasn't sure she wanted to hear his answer. Was certain she didn't want to hear him lie, but it needed to be asked.

"I'm not sure. I—" He looked down at his food, trying to gather his thoughts.

"You don't know how to act around me," she said. It was a statement, not a question.

He looked up at her. "I don't want you in my head."

He was afraid of her, afraid of her abilities.

"I'm not in your head," she assured him. "I can feel your resistance. I can feel you pushing me away. But I can't read your mind."

His relief was written all over his face.

"Tom." She reached across the table and laid her hand on his arm. "I want to save our marriage. But I don't want to live with secrets any longer. I don't want to hide who I am, and I don't want you to hide who you are, not from me. I understand you have a dangerous job, but you need to understand that I can handle it. I am Stuart Marster's daughter."

He winced as she said the name. "Don't do that. My dad might have gone a bit too far with his work, but only because he was committed to the agency and what they did. Kind of like you have been to your job."

He grinned and lifted his chin, his brown eyes twinkling in that way that first had her falling in love with him. "Okay, you got me there."

"I can take everything you have to offer. The question I'm asking is, can you take me? All of me."

He held her eyes for a long moment, and she felt him giving in. "All right. We'll do this together. Let's finish eating in the car; we need to hit the road. We can get a hotel in that small town at the bottom of the mountain and then head up to the estate first thing in the morning."

She shook her head. "No. I'm eating right now, and then I'm going to take a hot shower. I still have Anita's blood all over me. We can hit the road after."

"All right," he relented, taking another bite of Mongolian Beef. "But make it a fast shower."

13

They'd traveled late into the night and managed to get a few hours of sleep, then they sat down to a good breakfast and a strong cup of coffee. Tom had just taken his first bite when his phone rang. It was Sam. "Tom here," he said, looking at Cat across the table.

"Anita's gone," Sam said without preamble.

Tom stiffened and dropped his fork. "You're kidding? How?"

"We're not sure. There was an agent posted at her hospital room all night, but this morning when the nurses went in to change her dressing, she was gone."

"All right, keep me posted." Tom hung up the phone. "Anita is gone, and the FBI doesn't have a clue what happened."

Cat's eyes widened. "Do you think she left on her own, or does Carlos have her?"

He shook his head. "For her sake, I hope she left on her own."

"I noticed you didn't tell Sam where we were."

He looked down at his eggs, deciding how much to say, then remembered they were going to tell each other everything. He took a deep breath. "There were only a handful of people who knew about my conversations with Anita, and somehow Carlos still found out. And now she's gone. Again. I'm not taking any more chances."

"You don't trust him?"

"In this business, you can't trust anyone."

Her lips tightened. "I can see where a lot of our problems have been coming from."

"I've told you everything now."

"I appreciate that. Though I still don't know if we're going to be able to find a way to make this marriage work."

"I want to make it work."

"But not enough to commit to it."

He looked up from his eggs. He didn't need this right now. "I would say the fact that we're both here right now against my better judgment says how much I'm committed. Let's just get the book, turn it in, and go home. I'll take some time off so we can be a family again. See where that leaves us. Can we do that?"

"On one condition," she said, scooting around the booth so she was next to him.

He took a deep breath, trying to hold his frustration in check.

"I want you to kiss me."

He didn't expect that. His gaze held hers and his

chest tightened. "I think I can do that." He leaned over and kissed her. His lips touched hers. Softly at first and then she took over. Her arms wrapped around his neck as she deepened the kiss. Their lips parted and her tongue entered his mouth. Warmth filled him and he kissed her long and hard. For a moment, he wished he could forget this job. Forget Anita and her damned book, and just take Cat back to the room and make sweet love to her all morning.

Like he should have done last night.

Like he should have done many times over the years but hadn't.

He broke the kiss. "I'm sorry. I wish we could stay and spend some time together." He dropped his forehead against hers.

"Me, too." Her cheeks were flushed, her lips swollen.

"I would like to make love to you right now."

She smiled. "That's all I needed to hear. Unfortunately, we have a job to do and duty calls."

"It's nice having you with me."

"Of course, it is. We make a great team. We always have. We just lost sight of that."

"It won't happen again," he assured her and hoped he could keep that promise.

They got in the SUV and headed toward the Bodega estate, back onto the twenty miles of treacherous mountain roads. He parked the SUV off the main road and stared into the woods. "Are you sure about this?"

he asked Cat. "You can always go back to the motel and wait for me there."

"Don't worry about me." She held up the gun he'd handed her. "I can handle myself."

He tried not to cringe at the sight of her holding his extra firearm, but he couldn't help himself. They went in on foot, skirting through the trees. This time they had a pair of wire cutters so they could cut the fence when they neared the estate.

"Watch for cameras," she warned him. They seemed to be pointed at the drive every fifty feet.

"When we see one, let's knock it off target a bit instead of taking it out. I'd like to hide our presence as long as possible."

"Sounds good. Where did Anita say she put the book?"

"In her closet. Her rooms are in the wing opposite where they kept us."

"You mean on the other side of the estate?"

He nodded. They reached the area of the fence that was the closest to the house and spotted a camera straight above them. "Point it toward the ground and hopefully they'll think an animal did it."

"I'm going to need a boost," she said, looking at the camera about ten feet up in a tree.

Tom threaded his fingers together and bent over. She put her hand on his shoulder, then stood in his hands, balancing against the tall tree as he boosted her up high enough to reach the camera and tilt it toward the ground.

"Good job," he said as she jumped down.

They ran to the fence where he quickly snipped the wire, cutting an opening for them to slip through. They hurried across the drive toward the house, easing through the French doors to the bedroom they'd been in the day before.

Tom opened the door to the hallway and peered out. Everything was quiet. They crept down the hall and across the foyer to the opposite wing where Anita's rooms faced the back of the house.

"Where is everyone?" Cat whispered as they reached the end of the hall.

Tom shrugged and opened the door to Anita's room. They froze in the doorway. The suite of rooms had been destroyed. Mattress overturned and slashed, drawers emptied on the floor. Everything that had been on top of the dresser and nightstands was strewn in a broken pile on the floor.

"What are the odds the book is still here?" Cat asked.

"Let's check the closet." There were two closed doors in the far wall. Tom opened the first one. Not a closet but a workout room. An entire wall was a full mirror with a ballet bar in front of it. A far wall held ski and backpacking equipment, another with weights and exercise machines.

"Wow. I like this woman," Cat said in appreciation. "Look." She pointed outside the French doors to a private courtyard where a large climbing wall at least twelve feet high reached beyond the stucco walls.

"We need to find the closet." He left the room and opened the other door. Cat followed.

"This closet is as big as Mark's room back home." She winced as she took in the shredded clothes, empty jewelry boxes, tattered shoes, all Anita's possessions laid bare for everyone to see, take, and destroy.

Tom took a dime out of his pocket and started unscrewing the screws in the light switch. Once they were out, he pulled the plastic cover off the wall and reached inside around the receptacles.

"Got it." Tom retrieved a small book from the opening.

"That's it?"

"Yep. Carlos' little black book of drug pushers across the US." He shoved it into his back pocket. "Now, let's get out of here."

They walked out of the closet and into the main room just as Tony walked through the door flanked by two guards.

"I'll take that." He held out his hand.

"Take what?"

Tony's eyes narrowed. "Do you really want to play that game? I'm going to get the book. The question is how much pain do you want to endure first?" His dark eyes swung from Tom to Cat, then back to Tom again.

Tom had no choice but to give him the book. He pulled it out of his pocket and handed it to him.

"Thank you. My boss will be very happy we found it." He took a step back, placing the book in his inside jacket pocket.

"You have what you want, now let us go," Tom said.

Tony smiled. "You can go. She stays."

"Not a chance," Tom gritted through his teeth.

"We can have a go at round two if you want, but I'm more interested in the plaything you brought me." Tony's eyes moved over Cat.

"Touch her and you're dead." Terror rolled through Tom at the thought of what Tony and his thugs might do to Cat.

Tony smiled. "That sounds like a challenge."

Cat backed up.

Tony walked toward her. Tom started to move, to stop him, but the guards stepped forward, their raised guns pointed at him.

"How about you stay right there and watch how a real man treats his woman," Tony said, grinning and licking his lips.

Cat cowered away from him, her face crumpling in fear as her hands came up in front of her and tears filled her eyes. "Please don't touch me," she cried, sounding weak. Looking small.

Rage filled Tom. He moved toward her and felt one of the guards grab his arm and shove the barrel of the gun in his side. "Give me a reason, *amigo*. Any reason."

Tony smiled, obviously enjoying Cat's fear. He reached for her shirt, grabbing it and pulling, ripping the fabric.

Cat's eyes narrowed, her face hardening as she stepped back from him. "This is my favorite shirt." Before he could respond, she swung her leg and kicked

Tony square in the privates. Hard. Shock filled his face as Tony bent in two, groaning. She stepped forward and kicked him again.

"Stop, or I'll kill him," the guard yelled, shoving Tom forward.

Cat didn't listen. She grabbed Tony's head and brought it down on her raised knee. He cried out as blood gushed to the floor. The guard's eyes were riveted on Cat. Her face twisted in anger and hatred. She was ferocious as she used her elbows and knees, hitting all Tony's soft and vulnerable spots.

She was incredible.

The guard pulled his gun away from Tom, pointed at Cat, and fired just as Tom grabbed the barrel. The bullets hit the wall behind her. He jerked the gun and swung it around, shooting the guard behind him who had his rifle pointed at Cat, dropping him to the floor. Tom pivoted and shot the guard next to him, then turned to find Tony, a quivering bloody mess on the floor.

"Put him out of his misery," Cat ordered.

"What? He's down."

"We need to make sure he stays that way." He stared at her in astonishment as she pulled the gun he'd given her from her waistband and shot Tony in the heart. She was right, Tom knew that. He just didn't expect it. She reached inside Tony's jacket, pulled the book out of his pocket, and threw it to Tom.

With the guard's gun in his hand, he ran toward Anita's exercise room, grabbed the loaded hiking backpack off the wall, and slipped out the French doors into Anita's private courtyard. "That way," he said, pointing to the climbing wall.

Cat nodded and hurried toward it, scaling it like an expert, her small feet clutching the holds, her strong arms pulling her up quickly.

"How'd you learn how to climb?" he asked as he followed her footsteps.

"Do you know how many birthday parties I take the twins to at these places? I have to do something while they're on the kiddie walls."

He nodded in appreciation. "Impressive. So was the way you handled Tony."

"Yeah, I watch a lot of self-defense videos."

He took in her lithe form and easy movements, his eyes narrowing. "You don't expect me to believe that, do you?"

She grinned. "I sure hope not."

He was beginning to look at his wife in a whole new light, and he had to admit, he was intrigued. They got to the top of the wall and dropped down into the forest on the other side, then hurried into the trees and ran.

After a long while, they slowed to a walk. "Do you think Anita placed the climbing wall where she did just for that reason?" Cat asked.

"It's possible. And she had a bug-out bag loaded and ready by the door."

"A bug-out bag?"

He swiveled his shoulder and showed her the backpack on his back. "I don't know what's in it, but I'm sure whatever there is, we'll need it."

"Hopefully there's dinner and a bottle of wine."

He laughed and she gave him a smile that made his heart skip a beat. It had been a long time since he'd felt that skip. After all they'd been through and as crazy as their day had been, he didn't think he could have ever been more attracted to her than he was at that moment.

14

Several hours later Cat and Tom were deep in the forest and hadn't seen or heard another person. The sun started to sink in the sky as it exploded in a rainbow of colors, moving from pinks to deep reds.

"It's gorgeous here," Cat said, trying not to grumble about the multitude of mosquito bites along her arms and neck. Thank goodness she was wearing jeans and sneakers. "Any idea where we might be?"

"No, I thought we'd run into some kind of house or hunting cabin by now."

"I wonder how much of this land Carlos owns. That might be why."

"If we don't find something soon, we're going to need to find somewhere to camp for the night. We don't want to be walking out here in the dark."

Cat didn't like the sound of that. "I wonder how cold it gets at night." She was already starting to feel the chill.

"We'll light a fire."

That couldn't be good. A fire would let anyone looking know exactly where to find them. They continued west, hoping it would take them toward civilization when Tom pointed toward a rocky outcropping. "That looks like a good place to set up camp."

She followed him toward the large granite boulders. If they camped between them, it would offer protection on two sides, not only from the elements and any wild animals, but from Carlos' guards too. Those hired guns might be waiting for nightfall, waiting for them to light a fire that would pinpoint their location. She hoped these rocks would block the fire's glow.

They reached the boulders and walked down a steep slope beneath them. "They're much taller than I realized. This will be perfect." Tom circled them, looking for a place to set up camp.

"No. The Omni with its thousand-count sheets and hot running water would be perfect. Pine needles and giant boulders, not so much."

Tom grinned and dropped the pack and the gun, then started to collect small pieces of wood. Cat scouted the area nearby. There had to be water somewhere. She was dying of thirst but was afraid if she drank the water out here, it would make her sick. She checked her cell phone. Still no signal. Genie and Becca probably thought she was at the hotel having wonderful makeup sex with her husband. She chuckled at the thought.

"What is it?" He looked at her. His hair was mussed, and a streak of dirt lined his cheek.

"Nothing. Just wondering how long we can go without water. And food. I'm starving."

"Maybe we can catch a squirrel."

"A squirrel? You want me to eat a cute little rodent?"

He grinned. Obviously, he'd been teasing her. "How about collecting more wood for the fire? We'll want to keep it going all night."

Why, because otherwise we'd freeze to death? "Fine." She saw a log nearby and gingerly picked it up, then quickly dropped it as spiders scurried out from beneath it. She kicked at the log, then grabbed it by one end, cringing as she banged it on the ground until she was certain the spiders were all gone, then carried her prize back to the camp.

Tom was giving her that annoying little amused smile of his.

"What?"

"If you do that with every log, it's going to take a while."

"Sorry, if I don't want spiders, beetles, and god-knows-what-else crawling up my arm."

"It's the snakes you need to worry about."

She stared at him wide-eyed.

He laughed again. "Haven't you ever been camping?"

"Not real camping. We had a cabin on the island that we camped at, with running water, toilets, beds, and a refrigerator. Besides, Genie was the outdoor enthusiast. Not me."

"Oh, I don't know. The way you've been trekking all day, not to mention climbing mountains, I'd say you can handle yourself in just about any situation."

Her chest warmed with the compliment. "Thank you. I appreciate that." Smiling, she turned to find more wood, searching for branches that had recently fallen. As she ventured farther down the hill, she heard water running. She rushed toward the sound and found a bubbling creek.

She turned to call Tom but realized she'd walked farther than she thought. She didn't see him or the rocks they were camped beneath. There were so many tall trees. She walked back the way she came and suddenly could smell the fire. She followed the scent until she found the rocks and Tom.

"There you are," he said.

"I found a creek."

"Good. Anita's backpack has a sleeping bag and a small tarp. We can lay on the tarp and put the bag over us."

"Any food?"

"Granola bars and a few freeze-dried meals." He dug in the pack and handed her one of the bars.

She took it and tore it open. "Better than nothing."

"And there's pills so we can drink the water." He unhooked a large plastic water bottle from the side of the backpack. "How about you show me where this stream is."

They walked back down the hill toward the creek. "They're not going to stop looking for us, are they?"

"Not as long as I have the book. But I doubt they'll come out after dark. We're safe for now."

Cat wasn't afraid of a lot of things. She'd been trained from an early age how to take care of herself. To defend herself from anyone who might come after her. She'd kept up her exercises especially after she had children. She was a black belt and an excellent marksman. Yes, she could climb Half Dome and jump out of an airplane. But camping—not her thing.

Tom didn't know anything about that, and she couldn't decide if she trusted him with that side of herself or not. The Cat he thought he'd married was a Susie-homemaker, PTA president, and could make a mean apple pie. Would he still want her if he knew she could kick his ass? She shivered with the thought.

He looked at her, his eyebrows raised.

"It's cold."

He put his arm around her as they walked down the hill toward the stream. For a moment, she imagined they were on a stroll in the woods, enjoying nature and the brisk evening air, and not running from men who wanted to kill them. He stooped close to the stream and filled the water container. She cupped her hands in the water and washed the day off her face.

She looked up to find him smiling at her. "What?"

"Nothing."

They walked back up the hill to their camp where he added the water purification tablets to the water and gave the bottle a shake. "Should only take about a half hour, and then we can drink it." She snuggled under the sleeping bag, trying to get warm. He lay next to her and pulled her closer.

"I hope you're right about them waiting until morning. The smell of the fire is a dead giveaway."

He was silent for a moment. "I'm sorry I got you into this. I shouldn't have let you come."

"Believe me, you didn't have a choice."

He laughed and moved his hand up her belly and over her breast, his fingers playing with her nipples through her T-shirt.

"You picked a fine time to get frisky, mister. Couldn't you have tried this back at the hotel?"

"If I recall, you weren't this close and personal then."

She rubbed her bottom against him and smiled as she felt his erection grow through his pants.

He leaned over and kissed her. The touch of his lips was soft, his mouth lingering on hers. Expectation surged within her.

"I'm sorry for getting you involved in this," he said.

"I'm not." She rubbed her fingers across his broken nose. "I don't want to think about what might have happened to you if we didn't show up when we did."

"Neither do I." His gaze darkened, moving over her and settling on her breasts. She felt her nipples harden in response. It had been so long since he looked at her that way. With appreciation, with *desire*. And the funny thing was, she must look a mess.

His rough palm scraped over her nipple. Why was she even more aroused at the idea that he probably had as much dirt on his hands as she had on hers? Obviously, she was losing it. Especially when his hand molded itself around her breast, lifting it as he bent his head forward and took her nipple in his warm mouth.

Fire shot through her belly and she moaned softly, her breath quickening. He was gentle, taking his time getting to know her body all over again. She drew her fingers through the hair at his nape, playing with the curls. Her head fell back and pleasure moved through her. She clenched her legs together, holding it in, making it last.

They had always been so good together. What happened? Why had they stopped loving one another? He paused and stared at her. She took his head in her hands and pulled him down to kiss her. She swept her tongue into his mouth, their passion setting her blood on fire.

She held him so tight, she could barely breathe. But she didn't need to breathe; she only needed to hold on and never let him go. Feeling him against her, smelling his scent, tasting his warmth on her lips was all that mattered, all she needed.

Tears sprung to her eyes and she wasn't able to contain the emotion she was feeling at the moment—the relief that they were still alive, the love she felt for this man who'd been her husband for the last ten years, whom she almost lost.

Could still lose.

She leaned up and kissed him again, moving her hands up his shirt, rubbing them across his chest, playing with his nipples and feeling them tighten beneath her touch. He unbuttoned her jeans, pulling down her zipper, and yanking them off her hips. She used two hands to wriggle out of them as he took off his. He pulled his shirt off as she lifted hers over her head, then unhooked her bra and let it fall to the side.

Their hands moved over each other, their bodies melding together as need surged through them. She never tired of looking at Tom, of touching him. He was trim and fit, with beautiful muscular shoulders and thighs. His butt was tight, his abs defined. She could see why other women were attracted to him; she didn't blame them, but she wasn't sharing either.

His lips moved down her throat, tasting, suckling, devouring. Across her breasts, they lingered and enjoyed, inflaming her passion. Desire seeped through her, tightening her core as he licked the nubs of her breasts. And then he continued his exploration, moving down her belly.

She sucked in a breath of anticipation. She knew where he was going and what he planned to do. He settled between her legs, lifted them onto his shoulders, and kissed her, nibbling. Sending her worries and fears flying from her mind, and all she could think of was the fire growing within her.

She squirmed beneath his touch as his fingers delved deep inside her. "Oh, Tom," she cried as the sweet friction built between them. She arched her back, trying to move him closer, hoping he'd hit the sweet spot that would send her reeling.

He pulled back, settling on top of her. His hardness filling her sent ecstasy rushing through her body. He started to move, thrusting in and out, so fast and so deep that she cried out with absolute pleasure. A growl rumbled deep in her throat. She was so close to falling, but she liked where she was, dangling on the precipice where there was only the feel of their desire, the smell of their sex, the roar of her blood humming through her ears.

She clung tight, wrapping her long legs around his back, holding on to his shoulders as he moved within her—a rod of steel melting her from the inside out. She gasped deep breaths. "Yes, yes. Right… There."

She couldn't breathe.

Couldn't think.

He kept hitting that magic spot.

Harder.

Deeper.

Her heart was surely going to burst as she rose higher and higher until her lungs clenched and her entire body convulsed as an orgasm seized her. She cried out loud, biting down on her bottom lip. And then he stiffened, letting loose a primal yell. The cords in his neck tightened as he lost himself and collapsed on top of her.

Her heart started to beat once more, and she pulled in gasping, quaking breaths.

"I think I died," she said after a long moment.

Tom grinned. "You didn't die, darling."

"I did," she insisted.

"Then you are the most beautiful corpse I've ever seen."

She turned to him and smiled, the afterglow of their lovemaking filling her with mind-numbing pleasure. "Can we do that again?"

His brows raised. "I'm really trying to survive this day if you don't mind."

She patted him on the shoulder. "Rest for a few minutes, then you'll be fine."

He laughed out loud. "Who are you, and what did you do with my wife?"

15

Tom opened his eyes as dawn broke in the sky. He sat up and pulled on his shirt, then stepped into his jeans, covering Cat with the sleeping bag. He stared at her for a long moment. Her blond curls resting against her cheek, her lips slightly chapped. He recalled kissing those lips last night and smiled. It had been a long time since they'd loved one another like that. Too long. Maybe if they had, they wouldn't be in the difficult place they were in today.

He stoked the fire and placed another log in the ashes, then took the empty water bottle down to the stream to refill it. He pulled out the last of the food and hoped they'd find their way off the mountain today.

"Good morning," Cat said, opening her sparkling blue eyes and stretching her arms above her head.

"Good morning to you. What would you like for breakfast this morning? We have granola bars with almonds or granola bars with oats and honey."

"Hmm. Tough choice. I'll go with the granola bars with almonds."

He handed one to her. She smiled, got dressed, then tore open the package. "How many more miles before reaching the bottom of the mountain?"

"I have no idea," he admitted.

"Hopefully we'll find a farmhouse with a nice little old farmer who will give us a ride back to town."

"I wouldn't count on that. Not in these hills. Knocking on doors around here could land us in even deeper trouble. Why do you think we've never been able to find Carlos up here?"

She grimaced. "I'm going to go down to the stream and wash up."

"I'll clean up here. Be careful."

"I will." He watched her walk down the hill, then retuned the gear to the backpack, put out the fire, and tried to remove all trace of their presence. He slung the backpack over his shoulder and joined her at the creek. The two of them watched a mother deer and her two babies drinking downstream.

"It's almost beautiful enough to forget these mountains are filled with killers," Cat said as she washed her face, rinsed out the cloth, then gently washed his. He winced slightly. She grimaced. "Your poor nose will never be the same. I'm afraid your pretty-boy good looks are gone forever."

His eyes widened.

"Luckily, I think your new bad-boy look is even sexier."

He grinned. "Ouch." He pulled back.

"Yeah. Your lip is split too. Here." She leaned forward and kissed him gently. "Better."

Desire darkened his eyes. "Almost."

She smiled. "I don't know about you but a toothbrush and hot shower are in order, and the sooner the better."

He smacked her butt. She playfully turned from him and continued heading down the mountain. The Cat he was married to—mother, wife, the woman who made a killer lasagna and a beautiful home—was someone completely different than this Cat.

He had to admit as he watched her easy sway, she excited him.

And scared him at the same time.

They continued down the mountain for another two hours before stopping to take a drink from the water bottle.

"Any more granola bars?" she asked.

"Sorry, we ate them all."

"Bummer."

He was about to make another wisecrack about eating a squirrel when they heard the beep of a radio. He put a finger to his lips and peered around the redwood tree they were sitting under. Two of Carlos' men were walking straight toward them. They'd be on them any moment.

"Let's go." They took off running down the hill. The incline sharpened, and Tom skidded down the loose rocks of the slope. Cat was right behind him. She fell, picked herself up, and skidded again.

The guards were getting closer.

Tom slipped again and rolled down the incline. He caught his breath, got to his feet, and kept running. A shot rang out. The bark of a tree shattered next to him, a piece grazing his cheek. They had to get out of sight.

The thick shrubs at the bottom of the hill might provide cover. He half ran, half fell down the mountain, his momentum carrying him as he dove into the tangle of green leaves and branches, Cat right behind him.

"Are you okay?" he asked as they both lay on the ground gasping lungfuls of air. She nodded. He grabbed her hand, and they jumped up and ran, hunching over under the cover of greenery in the opposite direction he hoped the guards expected them to go. Soon, they saw the reason for the thick shrubs. The small stream they had been washing in had turned into a large river.

"We should cross it. They wouldn't expect us to," she said.

"Let's go." They plunged into the icy waters that rose to their waists halfway across. They had just made it to the other side and into the bushes when they saw the guards come into view.

Their pursuers looked around, then followed the river downstream at a quick pace.

Cat and Tom sat still as the men disappeared.

"Do you think they have a vehicle?" Cat asked.

"Yes, they must to have been able to get down here so fast. There has to be a road around here somewhere."

"Let's follow the river and see if we can find it."

A while later, Tom heard the sound of an engine. "This way. Hurry." They ran toward the sound, broke through the brush, and saw a small two-lane road ahead.

"I can't believe it. I've never been so happy to see pavement in my life," Cat said, looking up and down the road. "Which way do you think the town is?"

"I'm guessing to the west. Head toward the ocean."

They walked for an hour until suddenly they heard the sound of another engine.

"Hide in the trees," Tom said.

"By myself? I don't think so. Besides, it sounds different from the Jeeps."

Surprised by her insight, he smiled and they both ran out into the road as an older black Ford pickup truck came into view. They waved their arms over their heads to flag the driver down. A man with deep lines etched in his face looked at them warily, a cigarette hanging from his mouth as he pulled to a stop.

"Can you give us a ride to the nearest town?" Tom asked. "We'd be happy to sit in the back." He pointed to the bed of the truck.

"What are you doing out here?" the driver asked, looking at them with suspicion heavy in his eyes.

"Backpacking. Got lost." Tom laughed and shrugged. "We have no idea where we are."

"You shouldn't be out in these hills. It's all private property."

"I got that," Tom said. "Just hoping to get back to civilization."

"And a hot shower," Cat said and smiled at the man.

He stared at them for a long moment. "All right. Get in." He gestured his head toward the back of the truck. They hurried around and climbed into the bed.

"Thanks so much," Tom said, sitting in the back up against the cab. He pulled Cat next to him.

She snuggled close, smiling when he pulled her down flat into the bed.

"What's going on?" she asked, eyes wide.

"One of Carlos' Jeeps is right behind us."

16

THE DRIVER PULLED the truck down the main street of the small coastal town and stopped. Cat slowly lifted her head and looked around them. They were parked outside a two-story blue clapboard house with a sign out front that read Moonstone Inn Bed and Breakfast.

Before she could climb out of the bed, Tom placed a hand on her arm. "Check for Carlos' guards first."

She looked around. Not a single Jeep in sight. They climbed out of the truck's bed. "Thanks for the ride," she said to the craggy-faced man. He nodded and watched them hurry up the sidewalk.

"Let's stay here," Cat said, pointing to the Moonstone Inn. "It's so cute, and I'm dying for a shower."

"Let's keep going." Tom glanced over his shoulder at the truck that dropped them off. "Just in case." They continued down the street. "There's another B&B." Tom pointed to a yellow house overlooking the ocean.

They crossed the street and entered a small gate

built into the white picket fence surrounding the front lawn. The porch steps were flanked on either side by large hydrangea bushes in full bloom. Cat ran her hand across one of the pink blossoms as they ran up the stairs. Tom took a last look down the street before they walked inside.

They opened the door and saw an elderly woman sitting behind a dark wooden counter.

"Good afternoon," she greeted, setting down her needlepoint.

"We'd like a room, please," Tom said.

"Ocean or street view," she asked with a welcoming smile.

"Street view," Cat said quickly.

"Can I see your identification please?" the woman asked.

As Tom gave her the information she needed, Cat walked up to the window and watched the street, looking for any sign of Carlos' guards. The streets were filled with tourists eating ice cream cones and taking pictures of each other and the amazing view of the rocky Pacific.

There was a popular restaurant next door. All the outdoor seats were taken. Her stomach growled at the sight and the smell of grilling meat. "Does the restaurant next door deliver?"

"They do. Here's their menu." The woman pulled a piece of paper out from under the counter.

"Thanks. I'm starving," Cat said and took the menu.

"Your room is on the second floor. First door to the right at the top of the stairs."

"Thank you," Tom said, and they quickly headed up the stairs.

"How do burgers and fries sound?" Cat asked, perusing the menu. "Or they have chicken or salmon."

"Burgers sound great."

"Perfect." She took out her phone and placed the order. "Dibs on the shower."

He laughed. "All right, I'll go downstairs to wait for the food as soon as I call Sam and check in."

Cat stepped into the hot water and took an extra-long time shampooing her hair and washing her body. She couldn't remember the last time a shower felt so good. She just wished she had clean clothes to change into. She found a robe in the closet and put it on. Tom still wasn't back. She peeked out the window but didn't see him. She spotted a boutique across the street and sent him a quick text.

If the food hasn't come yet, can you run across the street and buy me some clean clothes? Don't forget underwear.

A moment later she saw him crossing the street and smiled.

She dialed Genie's number and quickly filled her in on everything that happened.

"Do you need us to come to get you?" Genie asked.

"Tom called his partner. He should be on his way."

"All right, keep me posted. Have you talked to Tom about our new project yet? I really hope you can be a part of it."

"Me, too. I haven't had the chance, but I will as soon as he gets back with our food."

"Okay, call me later."

"Will do. Thanks, Genie." Cat hung up the phone as Tom walked into the room, a shopping bag in one hand, the food in the other. The smell of burgers and fries filled the air. She grabbed the food from his hand.

He laughed. "I wondered which bag you'd take first."

"Go get in the shower," she ordered.

"Okay, but save me a burger."

She laughed and sat at the small table by the window and took out her food and tried to figure out the best way to tell him about her sisters' new endeavor. She didn't know how she and Tom would manage to be a part of it, but she wanted to try.

She scarfed down her burger, pretty certain she hadn't ever tasted anything that good. She had just taken the last bite when Tom came out of the shower, towel slung around his waist as he dug into the shopping bag, and pulled out a new pair of briefs and shirt.

"You're just in time. That other burger in the bag was about to be mine," she said with a grin.

He dropped the clothes. "That's a capital offense in my book." He reached into the bag and took the burger, unwrapped it, and took a huge bite. "This is a really good burger," he said with his mouth still full.

She laughed. "Right?"

She ate a fry and pulled out the clothes he bought

her. Lacy mauve panties and a very short sundress with spaghetti straps. She looked at him, eyebrows raised.

"What? I think you'd look fabulous in that."

"Well, at least you got the size right." She stood, slipped off the robe, and pulled the dress over her head. He was staring at her, his mouth open in mid-bite.

"You like?" she asked, warmth filling her chest. He hadn't looked at her like that in a very long time.

"Almost enough to stop eating this burger, throw you on the bed, and ravish you."

She grinned. "Then what's stopping you?"

"I need nourishment first." He took another huge bite and sucked down a quarter of his drink.

"Is Sam on his way?" she asked.

"He is. He was already on the road when I called. He'd been concerned when he couldn't get ahold of either one of us and luckily guessed where we were."

She held up her panties. "Are you done with that burger yet?"

"Don't you dare put those on." He quickly polished off the rest of the burger, finished his drink, then stood up.

"Why, Mr. Phillips, what on earth do you have planned?" she teased.

"The way I figure it, we have at least an hour or so before Sam gets here."

"Really? Did you want to go sightseeing? This looks like such a cute town."

He stood in front of her. "No, I don't." He leaned down and kissed her lips, pulling her up against his hard chest and devouring her. She twined her arms around his neck and melted against him.

He reached his hands down and cupped her bottom through her short sundress, caressing her skin with his palms and the tips of his fingers. Then he spun her around, leaned her over the bed, and flipped her dress up. The cool air hit her skin, and she knew he was staring at her.

"This is all I've been able to think about since I saw the dress hanging on the mannequin in the store's window."

He rubbed his hands across her bottom. "Spread your legs wider."

His command sent heat flooding through her. She did as he asked, anticipation kicking up her pulse. She sucked in a deep breath as he slid his hands between her legs. Fire shot through her as he rubbed her tender skin.

Tom was always a gentle lover, reserved, considerate. This was not the Tom she was used to. He roughly slipped his fingers into her sex, pushing them deep, then pulled them out and rubbed her nub. She groaned with pleasure. Lord, she wanted him to take her just as she was. Now.

She rubbed her bottom against him. His towel dropped; his erection was hot and hard. She felt him probing. "You want this?" he asked.

"Oh, God, yes!"

He grabbed her hips and in one quick movement plunged inside her. She cried out with pleasure as he started to move. Thrusting hard and fast, her body melting beneath him. She gripped the blankets, trying to hold on to something, even as she was quickly losing control.

The sound of their bodies slapping against each other filled the room in chorus with their heavy breathing and tortured moans. For a moment, she hoped the sound of their lovemaking wasn't filling the halls of the small house, even as he drove into her welcoming body—fast, hard, deep.

She cried out as her orgasm quickly took her, her insides clenching around his cock until he yelled, pushing her down and collapsing on top of her as his release rocked them both and his seed shot inside her.

If she were still able to have children, that right there would have done it, she was certain. He was buried so deep within her, she couldn't move. Didn't want to. Didn't want this moment to end.

They lay on top of each other, then they both started to laugh. "It must be the adrenaline," Tom said.

"Must be," Cat agreed. "If so, I think we need to work together more often."

He rolled off of her, lying on his side, looking at her. "You do? How would that work?"

"My sisters and Cameron have started a new department within the CTA. They are charged with finding subjects from my father and Tom Garrison's experiments. Discover if they need help and if they do, invite them to join our team. Genie and Kyle have turned my dad's estate in the Puget sound into a training facility. They want to teach the recruits how to control their abilities and provide agent training too."

Tom's eyes widened. "They're turning people with abilities into agents?"

She grinned. "We do make great agents."

He sat up. "You're serious about this?"

"Yes, Tom. I think we make a great team. It would be fun. Different. Exciting. Come do this with me."

"My job is in New York. My family is there. Our home. What about the kids' school?"

"Tom, we could make it work. You know that."

He stood as he started pulling on his clothes.

"What is it that is bothering you? I'd like to do this. I don't want to go back to being the perfect housewife. I want more from my life."

"You are a mother, Cat. Are you tired of that too?"

She got to her feet, instantly annoyed. "I can do both, Tom. You do both. Or are you tired of being a father? Is that why you're hardly ever home?" She reached for him with her mind. Wanting to know how he really felt, wanting to make sure she could trust him. Then she stopped herself. She couldn't cross that line. Once she did, the trust would be gone and their marriage over.

"That's not fair," he said. "Being an FBI agent is my job."

"And now I'm being offered a job, too. A job I could be good at. We can live in the house I grew up in. The kids would love it, and there is a great school on the island. I want this, Tom. I want the kids to get to know their aunts."

He picked up his phone off the table and looked at it, though she didn't hear it beep.

"Sam's almost here. I'm going to meet him downstairs. I need a moment to think."

He just lied to her, she thought as she watched him walk out the door, her heart sinking. He wasn't going to change his life and come with her. He was going to make her choose. She finished getting dressed. She needed to take a walk. To clear her head.

There was a knock on the door.

She quickly opened it, hoping he changed his mind.

Two of Carlos' guards stood in the doorway, a single long-stemmed rose clutched in one of their hands. "Carlos says hello."

17

Tom walked up and down the streets, circling the town and back again, trying to figure out what he was going to do. Cat's abilities were amazing, and so were her sisters'. He could see why the CTA would authorize a splinter group comprised of agents with special abilities, but he didn't feel comfortable around them.

He was going to have a hard enough time looking at Cat the same way after all of this once life got back to normal. *If it got back to normal.* How could he possibly be around her and her sisters, not to mention a school full of others, all working on their abilities? *All the time.*

And what about his job at the FBI? Was he supposed to give up his career and everything he'd worked for his whole life, just because she wanted to play agent with her sisters? He couldn't do that. But would she go without him? The thought tightened his chest. Last week, he would have told anyone that his wife put their family above all else. He didn't believe that anymore.

One thing this weekend had taught him, his wife was not the woman he thought she was. He really had no idea who she was at all. He thought of Cat demanding that he kill Tony, her expert fighting and shooting skills. The way she scaled that wall as if she were Spiderman. No, she could never go back to making cupcakes and selling fundraiser tickets for the PTA. Those days were behind them.

She would never be happy with the way things were. But would he be happy with this new brave Cat? She was no longer going to hide who she was. He had to love all of her—including a Cat with special abilities. Could he do that?

The fact that he had been hiding a huge part of his life from her too wasn't lost on him. Their marriage would definitely be different. But would it be for the better? He could still taste her kiss on his lips. One thing was certain, his body wasn't ready to let her go, and neither was his heart.

He saw Sam pull up and park and walked toward him. "Thank you for coming."

"Of course." Sam looked up and down the picturesque street. "Nice place."

"Any word on Anita?" Tom asked.

"No, we still don't know what happened to her. Whether Carlos has her, or she left on her own. No one saw anything."

"No surveillance footage?"

Sam shook his head. "Nothing revealing."

"I'd be surprised if she could make herself disappear

so easily," Tom said, but as he thought of the bug-out bag and the climbing wall in her room, maybe she was more prepared than he thought.

"Do you have the book?" Sam asked.

Tom grinned. "I do. Let's go get Cat and get back to the city. I'm ready to put this place and this case behind us and go home."

"You got it."

They went into the B&B and hurried up the stairs. Tom opened the door as he got to the room, but Cat wasn't inside. Lying on the crumpled bed was a note and a single long-stemmed rose.

He rushed to the bed and picked up the note.

Your wife and her sisters are some of the most beautiful women I've ever seen. I've decided to add them to my collection.

Carlos

18

Cat woke up to pain throbbing through her skull.

What happened?

Then the memories flooded into her mind. Carlos' guards. They used chloroform on her. Smart. Otherwise, they wouldn't have been able to take her. She kept her eyes shut and tried not to move as she reached out around her with her senses. Three guards. The whine of an engine. Jostling. Her back tweaked and spasmed. She needed to stretch but was afraid to move.

She must be in the rear of the Jeep. *Where were they taking her?* Certainly not back to the estate. Did they have Tom, too?

Cat! Genie!

She reached for her sisters with her mind but didn't feel anything. They were too far, and she wasn't strong enough.

What was Carlos going to do with her?

The book. That's all he wants. He'll call Tom for an

exchange.

Unless he already has Tom.

"The boss wants an ETA," one of the guards said.

"Tell him fifteen more minutes."

"*Muy Bonita señora* won't be so pretty after a month in his pits. I wouldn't mind some time with her before we put her on the plane."

The pits? Cat shuddered at the images that word invoked.

"No time," the other guard said.

"I won't take long, *amigo*." The man laughed.

A moment later, the Jeep pulled to an abrupt stop. Horror seeped through Cat's bones as she realized what they were planning to do.

The door opened, and she felt a hand on her arm pulling her out of the Jeep. She hit the ground with a vicious thud. She opened her eyes as pain pierced her head and back. Two guards descended on her, wicked lascivious grins on their faces as they unhooked their belts.

"Come on, pretty lady. You treat us nice, and we'll be nice to you," one guard said, unfastening his pants and pulling down his zipper. His dark gaze accented by heavy brows moved over her bare legs, exposed by her short dress that was flipped up over her panties.

Cat quickly scrambled to her feet. "Leave me alone," she cried while she desperately tried to form a plan.

"Sorry, we can't do that," the other guard said, obviously enjoying the show. "But don't worry, we won't take too long. The boss is waiting for his turn."

"What will Carlos say when he hears you damaged the merchandise?"

"We'll tell him you fought us," the guard with the heavy brows said. "So, please. Go ahead. Fight us." He reached for her.

"Then I have no choice," she said with as much bravado as she could muster.

"To do what?" he asked sarcastically.

"To fight you." She balled her fist.

The man chuckled and looked over at his compadre. "I like a woman with a little fight in her." He grabbed his dick and gave it a good rub. "Makes me *caliente.*"

He turned back to her, and she kicked him in the balls as hard as she could. He cried out and bent forward. "Why do men always leave that place wide open?" She kicked again, this time doing a roundabout, her foot connecting with the side of his head.

He fell to the ground but before she could go at him again, the other guard called out, "Stop right there." His rifle was aimed at her, the snide smile now gone from his face.

"I don't think Carlos would like it if you kill his prize."

"He'll understand."

"I'm pretty sure he won't." Taking a chance, she turned and bolted into the woods, running as fast as she could. He took off after her, but he wasn't as fast, or as agile in his boots, and carrying a heavy rifle.

She ran downhill with no idea where she was or

how she could find Tom. She just hoped he was okay. She kept running, pushing through the trees and bushes, their branches scratching her bare legs and arms. She hardly noticed them as she flew down the slope, unaware of how much time had passed until she stopped and bent over, clutching her knees and gasping for breath.

After a moment, her breathing returning to normal, she stilled to listen. She didn't hear the guard who'd been chasing her. No matter what, she couldn't let them put her on that plane. If she did, no one would ever find her. She was pretty sure she'd rather be dead than in the pits.

She stood upright and took a look around but didn't see anything but trees. The sound of a bullet split the air. She bent down and ran again, zigzagging her way down the mountain, trying to make sure she wasn't an easy target for a sniper's rifle. Fifteen minutes later, she found a building. She stopped and ducked down behind a bush.

No more bullets whizzed by her, and she didn't hear footsteps breaking through the brush. Hopefully, she lost him. She eased out from behind and cautiously circled the building, staying out of sight until she reached the front and could see inside. She froze as she heard voices speaking in Spanish.

An engine roared to life and her heart dropped as a large truck towed a plane out the building's doors.

Son of a bitch!

She'd run straight to Carlos' hangar.

19

Tom dropped the note and ran from the room, taking the stairs two at a time. He bolted through the lobby, crashed out the front door, and down to the street. Neither Cat nor Carlos' guards were in sight. He stood for a moment, scanning the street, the sidewalks, parking lots, and cars. Searching for any sign of them but finding none.

He returned inside to ask the woman at the front desk if she saw Cat leave, but she wasn't there.

"Anything?" Sam asked, approaching him, Carlos' note in his hand.

Tom shook his head, his gaze fixated on the note.

"I've called headquarters," Sam said. "A team is on the way."

"They'll never make it in time." Tom turned toward the front desk. "Hello," he called out, looking for the woman who ran the inn. Someone had to have seen something. He saw the tip of her shoe, rushed forward, and found her lying in a heap on the floor behind her desk.

He dropped to her side and felt for her pulse. She was alive but out cold. He pulled out his phone and called 9-1-1. "I have an unconscious woman on the floor at the Main Street B&B." He stood and turned to Sam. "The paramedics are on their way. Let's go."

Tom hurried out the door, Sam following close behind as they ran toward Sam's car.

"Where are we going?" Sam asked as he started the engine.

"To Carlos' estate in the mountains. I can't think of anywhere else he might have taken her. You drive while I study the satellite photos. If there's an airstrip, he probably has her there."

They drove in silence for a minute while Tom studied the images. "I don't see anything."

"We should wait for backup," Sam said. "There are too many guards for just the two of us."

"Even if they flew here, it would take at least two hours. By then, Cat would be on her way to Columbia." He shook his head. "I don't understand how they knew where we were. No one knew. No one except…" Tom turned to Sam as suspicion clouded his thoughts. "Tell me it wasn't you."

Sam looked at him, then did a double take. "What? No!"

"No one else knew where we were. No one."

"It wasn't me," Sam insisted. "You know me. We've

been partners for years. I would never…" He shook his head. "How could you even think that?"

Tom looked at him and suddenly wished he could sense the truth from him, wished Cat was here to tell him what she felt. He couldn't believe she was gone. That he'd lost her. Anxiety crashed over him.

"I can't lose her, Sam."

"You won't. We'll get her back."

Tom could hear the doubt in his partner's voice. Carlos' guards had her. Who knew what those animals would do. Why had he brought her out here with him? He knew better, but he'd let her convince him she would be all right. That she could handle herself. He'd been an idiot, and now she was gone. Lost to him.

And to his children.

How would he face Mark and Annie? They needed their mother. He had to find her. Even if he had to call the CTA and her sisters to do it. He hated to admit it, but he needed them.

He took out his phone and dialed. "Becca, it's Tom. They have Cat."

"They what? Who?" Her voice rose in pitch.

"Carlos' men. We've returned to the estate, and they have Cat."

"What? I don't understand. We left you in San Francisco."

"I know. I'm sorry. We came up here to get the book. We were told Carlos had left and thought we could get in and out without anyone being the wiser. I never should have brought her with me." His throat tightened and he had to pause. "I'm sorry. We got the book, escaped, and were in a B&B in the little town at the bottom of the hill waiting for the FBI when Carlos' men got hold of her. I don't know where she is." He pulled in a deep breath.

"Tom, you need to do whatever it takes to find Cat. Give Carlos that damned book."

"I will. I promise." That went without saying. "But I'm not sure it will be enough."

"I'm too far away to be of any help, but I'm calling Genie. Get my sister back."

"I will do everything I can." He hung up the phone. The moment he did, it rang again.

"Mr. Phillips?"

Tom recognized the accented voice instantly. "Where's my wife?"

"She's right here next to me. Sleeping," Carlos said.

Tom's grip tightened on the phone. "You will not touch her."

"You are in no position to make demands."

"What will it take to get her back? Unharmed."

"I think you know what. You will meet me at my house in thirty minutes with the book. If you don't, your lovely Cat will be flown to my estate in Columbia where she will be thrown into the pits along with my wife to service my men. Believe me, this is not an idle threat."

"Fine. Anything you want. Just don't hurt her. I'm on my way."

"Thirty minutes. Not a moment longer." Carlos disconnected the line.

Tom hung up the phone and debated what to do. He turned to Sam. "Did you hear?"

Sam nodded. "You can trust me. I'm not working with Carlos."

"I'm sorry I… I'm just upset." Tom called Genie.

"Did you find Cat?" she asked as she answered.

"I see you've spoken to Becca."

"I have. Kyle and I are already on our way."

"Good. Carlos just called. He wants an exchange. The book for Cat."

"And you trust him to keep his word?"

"Not for a minute. He's given me thirty minutes. We'll be there in fifteen."

"We're going to need more time," Genie said. "Where is the exchange supposed to take place?"

"At his estate."

"If you go there alone, he'll kill you both and take the book."

"I have no choice. Death would be preferable to what he has planned for Cat at his place in Columbia. If he gets her on his plane, we'll never see her again."

"All right, do what you have to. We'll be there as soon as we can."

"Thanks, Genie." He hung up the phone as Sam's car surged up the mountain. "My rental is still up there, parked alongside the road past the drive to his house. Drop me there, then you can return to town and wait for backup."

"You want me to leave you? No way."

"Come on, Sam. You and I both know I'm not getting out of that house alive. No reason for us both to go in."

Sam looked at him. "What about your kids?"

"How could I ever face them again if I didn't do everything I could to bring their mother home? It's a chance I have to take."

"You're my partner. What kind of agent would I be if I let you go in alone?"

"A smart one."

Sam was silent for a long moment. As they turned the bend, the old black Ford pickup truck was parked across the road. Sam hit the brakes and they screeched to a stop. "What the hell?" Sam yelled.

The craggy-faced man who'd picked Tom and Cat up earlier that day leaned against his truck, a cigarette hanging out of his mouth. Tom's stomach dropped.

"Un-fucking-believable," Tom muttered.

"I take it you know this guy?" Sam asked.

"Yeah, and now I know how Carlos learned where we were staying." Tom got out of the car and walked toward him. "Let me guess, you work for Carlos."

"In a manner of speaking," the man said. "I don't work for him, but he pays me well to do a few jobs here and there. And right now, he wants me to give you a ride up to his house. Alone." He looked pointedly at Sam.

"Great." Tom turned to Sam. "Thanks for your help. I'll take it from here."

Sam shook his head. "Don't do this. There has to be another way."

"I can't take the chance, not with Cat's life."

Sam got into his car, then turned around and drove down the mountain. Tom checked his gun in his waistband and turned back to man.

"Sorry to hear about that pretty wife of yours," he said, actually sounding sincere.

Tom looked at him in disgust. Never before had he just wanted to pull his gun and shoot someone with no provocation, but he did now. "Any idea where Carlos is keeping her?" Tom asked, knowing it was futile. There would be no help coming from this guy.

"Even if I did, I couldn't tell you. Can't take the chance. I have family here too. A wife and daughters I want to keep safe."

Tom shook his head and walked around the front to get into the passenger seat. "Good luck with that. You don't even want to know what Carlos has planned for my wife, or his for that matter."

The man nodded and he got behind the wheel. He was silent for a long moment, then looked at him as he started the engine. "Rumor has it, there is an airstrip down the mountain behind his place with a large hangar where he keeps his private jet. It's camouflaged very well. If he's planning on taking your wife out of the country, she'll probably be there. But you didn't hear it from me."

Tom wondered how he was going to get down there without Carlos and his guards seeing him. "I'm going to leave my phone on the seat. It doesn't get any service up here anyway, but when you get to town, if you could call the last number I dialed and tell the woman on the other end of the line what you just told me, we might have a shot of rescuing her."

"I don't know. That's taking a huge risk."

"Carlos won't find out. The woman is my wife's sister. I don't expect to make it out alive, but if there's a chance they can save my wife, I'll take it. Carlos is threatening to take her to Columbia. To throw her in a pit for his guards to use however they see fit. That man is an animal. Please, I'm asking as a father. We have two young kids at home who need their mother."

The man parked the truck in front of the estate. He didn't say anything as Tom got out, leaving the phone on the seat where he'd sat. The man took the phone and slipped it under the seat. Tom nodded his thanks and prayed he'd do the right thing, then turned and walked toward the house.

The door to the estate opened. Tom stepped behind one of the Jeeps parked in front, trying to use it for cover. "I want to see my wife," he yelled as the truck pulled away and disappeared up the drive.

Carlos walked toward him, an armed guard on either side. "I want my book."

Tom pulled it out of his pocket and held it up in the air. "You bring Cat to me and let us leave, and you can have your book."

"Or I can put a bullet in your head right now and take it," Carlos said with a grin.

"You're assuming I came alone," Tom said.

"I know you came alone. I saw you drive up with Henry. Don't forget, I have cameras on every inch of my estate."

"The FBI is on their way. I suggest we do this and do it quickly," Tom said, grasping at straws. "I don't care about your organization; all I want is my wife."

Carlos walked closer. "Hand me the book, Mr. Phillips, and I'll let you leave."

Tom took out the gun. "I'm not going anywhere without my wife."

"You have no choice in that matter. I no longer have your wife." He looked at the two guards on either side of him, both sporting black eyes and bloody noses. "My guards appear to have lost her. But that doesn't mean we won't find her again."

"Then we have no trade." Tom shoved the book into his pocket and took a step back. Cat was out there somewhere. They still had a chance.

"Of course we do," Carlos barked. "My book for your life."

The guards raised their weapons, pointing them at him. He wouldn't be able to hit both of them. He had no choice but to do as the bastard asked. He pulled the book out of his pocket and tossed it at the bastard's feet. Carlos picked it up, opened it, nodded in satisfaction, then turned toward the estate. He flipped through the pages as he walked toward the house. As soon as he stepped inside the front door, he turned and said the words Tom had been dreading.

"Kill him and find his woman. We're leaving within the hour." The door slammed shut.

Tom aimed and fired, hitting one of the guards square in the forehead. He dropped, the other guard running forward, firing at the Jeep. A shot rang out from the woods, and the other guard fell to the ground. Tom ran toward the trees, knowing more guards would be coming.

"My car's this way." Sam appeared next to him.

"Boy, are you a lifesaver." Tom followed him through the brush as they heard the shouts from Carlos' guards.

"I wasn't about to let you come down here alone. Where's Cat?" he asked as they continued up the hill toward the road.

"Carlos' guards lost her. At least that's what they told him."

"You don't believe them?" Sam asked.

"I think they'd say anything to keep from getting a bullet between the eyes. The man has everyone doing his bidding out of fear. But I've also seen Cat in action. If anyone could escape those goons, it's her."

"Then there's a good chance she's still out there. We'll find her."

Hope filled Tom for the first time since he found the note. They stopped next to a large boulder and looked around them. No guards were following. "How do you feel about searching for that hangar?"

Sam peered around the boulder. "The fact that someone in the San Francisco field office claimed the satellite footage showed Carlos already leaving on his plane, tells us someone we've been working with is on his payroll."

"Which means there's a good chance Carlos knows exactly when the FBI will get here."

"Then maybe he won't wait around to find Cat. We need to find her." One thing this weekend had taught him was that he wanted to fight for his marriage. "Cat!" he yelled, hoping she was out there somewhere.

Sam whipped around. "I understand the impulse, buddy, but all you're doing is letting the guards know where we are."

"Bring them on. Let's go."

20

Cat stopped running and tried to slow her breath and listen. She could swear she heard Tom calling her name. But that couldn't be possible. Could it? She started again, jogging in the direction of where she thought the sound had come from, hoping she'd hear it again.

She was tempted to call for him, but she couldn't take the chance. She wanted to get as far from Carlos' hangar as she could. Hopefully he'd get on his plane when he didn't find her and fly away. It was getting late and the last thing she wanted was to spend another night in these woods alone. Without Anita's sleeping bag, she'd freeze in this skimpy little sundress. "Come on, Tom. Call me again."

Then she heard a whistle. The same whistle he used to call the kids in for dinner. She smiled. It *was* him. She turned again, racing toward the sound. Unable to contain her excitement any longer, she took a chance and let out a loud whistle of her own.

Another whistle answered.

Closer this time.

With a huge grin on her face, she burst through the trees, and then she saw him. Without slowing, she barreled into his chest, jumping into his arms. She threw her arms around his neck and lifted her legs around his middle. He spun her around, squeezing her tight.

"Are you okay?" he asked, lifting her hair back to look at her.

"I am now." She buried her face under his chin. "Are you all right? What are you doing here?"

"Rescuing you."

She set her feet on the ground and gave him a high five. "Good job."

"Thank you." He grinned, emotion heavy in his eyes.

She tensed as she heard someone pushing through the brush, then relaxed when she saw it was Sam. "Hi, Sam."

"Good to see you," he said and pulled a twig out of his hair. "We better get moving. Half the mountain heard you two whistling."

"I'm pretty sure the road is this way," Tom said and then led the way.

"I have no idea where my car is," Sam grumbled as the sun sank lower in the sky.

"I can't believe you guys found me," Cat said, still grinning.

"Carlos offered to trade you for the book," Tom said.

"He did? Did you give it to him?"

"Of course. That's when I found out he lost you and knew we still had a chance to make it out of this."

"Sorry about the book, but I'm happy you found me."

"Me, too. All that matters is that you're safe." He wrapped his arms around her shoulders as they walked, and she snuggled close to him. "I was so scared I'd lost you."

"You're not losing me," she told him.

He stopped walking and dropped his lips over hers and kissed her, his tongue sweeping into her mouth.

"Can you guys continue that once we get off this mountain?" Sam asked.

"Spoilsport," Tom answered, and they hurried to catch up to him.

Not much farther, they found the road.

"What do you think? Should we go up the mountain to find my car or down toward town?" Sam asked.

"Whichever is closer," Cat said.

Tom looked both ways. "Hard to know, but down is easier."

They hiked until they heard the sound of a car approaching. A moment later that familiar old and battered pickup truck came rumbling toward them. It slowed to a stop. That same craggy-faced driver leaned out the window. "You guys need a ride?"

"No, thanks, I think we'll walk," Tom said, surprising Cat.

"It's ten miles to town," he said around his cigarette.

Tom took a step back, pulling her with him. "You told me you work for Carlos. We're not taking any chances."

The man shrugged. "Suit yourself."

"Wait," Cat said, stepping toward the truck. "We would love a ride."

"What?" Tom reached for her and pulled on her arm. "Cat…"

She turned to him. "It's okay. I trust him." She winked and grinned.

Tom stared at her for a moment; realization that she'd read the man's intentions entered his eyes. "Okay, if she trusts you, then I guess you're good."

Sam shrugged as he followed Cat.

The old man held Tom's phone out the window. "Here's your phone back. I made the call."

"Thank you." Tom accepted his phone, then followed them into the bed of the truck.

"What was that about?" Cat stared at his phone.

"I asked him to call Genie."

"You did? Is she coming?"

"Yes. Once we get down the hill and get cell service, we'll call her and tell her you're safe and find out where she is."

Cat smiled. "Tell her we're both safe." They held each other tight all the way down the mountain. When the truck pulled to a stop in front of the B&B,

two FBI agents were standing on the porch waiting for them.

"Thanks for the ride," Tom said as they climbed out of the bed of the truck. "And for all your help."

"You're welcome. I really hope Mr. Bodega is gone for good."

"Me, too," Tom said. "But I wouldn't count on it."

Just then, Genie came rushing out the front door of the B&B and ran down the stairs. "Cat!"

Cat ran into her arms and hugged her tight. "I can't believe you're here."

"Only because those FBI agents wouldn't let us storm the mountain. I wasn't going to let you stay up there alone much longer."

"Good to hear. It's starting to get cold."

"Well, duh, look at what you're wearing," Genie said, laughing.

Cat looked down at the torn and tattered sundress and cringed. "Please tell me you brought some extra clothes."

"Of course. Come on. Let's get you cleaned up."

As Cat followed her sister into the B&B, she looked back at Tom talking with Sam and the other FBI agents. After a moment, the men turned from the house and got into a vehicle. Without a backward glance, they drove up the road.

"Where's Tom going?" Genie asked.

Cat shrugged. "He just left with the other agents. They're probably going after Carlos and the book."

"Without telling you?"

"Appears so."

"I'm sorry. Men are just so…"

"Idiotic?" Cat grinned as Kyle walked into the room.

"Exactly," Genie said.

"Exactly what?" Kyle asked, flipping through a stack of menus in his hand.

"Nothing, babe," Genie said with a smile and gave him a quick kiss.

"You hungry?" Kyle asked.

"Starved," Cat said. "Give me ten minutes."

21

Tom and the others drove up the mountain where they met with two other carloads of agents who were already at the estate. Carlos and his plane were gone. Anything incriminating had been cleaned out of his office, and most of his guards had disappeared. There was no sign of Anita or what had happened to her.

Tom hoped for her sake that she had been able to escape. The worst part was admitting to his boss that he had the book Mrs. Bodega had promised but gave it back after Carlos took his wife. Cat shouldn't have been with him in the first place. They would place him on suspension pending a review. There were a lot of dead guards on the premises he had to answer for, after all.

He quickly sent a text to Cat letting her know he needed to go back to San Francisco with the other agents and write up his reports.

That's fine. I'm going to the island with Genie. I hope you'll meet me there.

He rode back to the city with Sam, sleeping most of the way. He had a big decision to make and needed a clear head to do it. It was after midnight when Sam woke him.

"We're at the Omni. Let's get some sleep. We'll go into the office and give our statements in the morning."

They walked into the hotel but after sleeping for so long, Tom was hungry. "You want to get a drink?"

Sam shook his head. "Too tired. I'll see you tomorrow."

"All right. Thanks for everything you did for me and Cat today."

Sam nodded as he stepped into the elevator. "That's what partners are for."

The doors slid shut, and Tom hoped Sam didn't hold his momentary doubt against him. He walked into the hotel's bar, took a seat, and ordered a drink along with their prime bites and house chips. Luckily, they were still serving.

"Mr. Phillips?"

Tom turned, surprised to see Anita standing behind him. "You're here. And safe." He looked beyond her to see if she was with anyone, but she was alone.

She nodded and smiled. "Do you want to get a table?"

"Sure." Tom slipped off the barstool and followed her to the far end of the room away from the windows. She was wearing jeans and sneakers, her hair in a ponytail that swung through the hole in the back of an SF Giant's ball cap. She looked nothing like the woman he'd seen there only a few days earlier.

She looked happy.

"It's good to see you," he said. "Did you want to get something to eat?"

"No, thanks."

"And your sisters?"

"They're safe too. Thanks to you and Mr. Wagner."

"I'm glad to hear it. What happened to you in the hospital?" he asked. "We were concerned Carlos found you again."

"Carlos' men were there. I saw them talking to one of the nurses. I knew they would take me back to Columbia, so I had to disappear. I'm sorry I didn't tell anyone, but I wasn't sure who I could trust. My husband can be a very ruthless man."

He remembered Carlos talking about his pits and shuddered. "I'm happy you got away. What are you going to do now?"

"The FBI has arranged to place me and my sisters into the witness protection program. I'm supposed to fly back to New York with Mr. Wagner tomorrow."

"That's wonderful news."

"Will you be coming with us?" Her green eyes locked on his and he saw the invitation there.

"I think I'm going to be stuck here most of the day. I have a lot of explaining to do, and then I need to find my wife and make things up to her. She's been through hell these last couple of days."

She nodded with understanding. "She's a very brave woman."

"She's incredible," he admitted and smiled with pride. It occurred to him at that moment that he couldn't wait to get back to her. To figure out what their new future was going to look like. One thing he knew for certain, it would be different from their past.

Anita smiled. "I just wanted you to know how much I appreciate everything you did for me." She took some folded papers out of her purse and slipped them across the table.

He unfolded them. They were photocopies of a list of names.

"I didn't get them all," she said. "But I was able to take a few pictures of the book with my phone before Carlos' men came for me. I hope they will help you."

He stared down at the two hundred plus names. Just names. No locations. But it was a start.

"This will help a lot." And go a long way to pulling his butt out of the fire. "Thank you."

"You're welcome." She stood, leaned down, kissed his cheek, then walked away.

He watched her go, then looked back down at the pages, a smile breaking out on his face. "We got you, Carlos, you bastard."

Tom finished his meal, then went up to his room. As he walked in the door, he was surprised to find Cat sitting on the bed waiting for him.

"You're here." Tom walked over to the bed and held out his hand. She took it and stood, then he pulled her into his arms. "I'm so glad." He couldn't stop touching her. Feeling her warmth seeping through his clothes. He kissed her lips, his mouth playing over hers. She felt warm, tasted sweet. His blood heated and pooled in his groin.

"I thought maybe we could see how we felt without the extra push of adrenaline surging through us," Cat said.

"You think I won't want you as much without all the excitement?"

She smiled. "It crossed my mind."

"What do your senses tell you?"

She wiggled against his erection and smiled. "That you're happy to see me."

"I am." He tilted his forehead to hers. "You are what is important—you and our family. I'm sorry I lost sight of that."

Tears filled her eyes. "I love you. I never stopped loving you."

"I'm a lucky man," he said, then picked her up and took her to bed.

EPILOGUE

Cat sat in a lounge chair next to the pool and watched Tom play in the water with Mark and Annie.

"Are you guys ever coming out?" Genie asked as she walked toward them a tray in her hands. She placed it on the table and took a chair next to Cat. "I brought chips and sandwiches."

"Auntie Genie, we're going to stay in until our skin falls off," Annie yelled and held up her shriveled fingers.

"Oh no, not that! I will never be able to find your skin again," Cat yelled with mock horror which sent the kids into a fit of giggles.

"They are having so much fun," Cat told Genie. "I wish Mom and Dad were here to see it."

Genie took her hand and squeezed it. "This place needs children in it again to chase all the bad memories away. Do you think Tom will want to stay?"

Cat watched him playing with the kids. "I don't

know. Sam's been in charge of building the case against Carlos and has asked him to come back once his suspension is over."

Genie grimaced. "Uh-oh."

"Tell me about it. I've been walking on eggshells waiting for him to make up his mind and trying not to push." Cat took a deep breath. "Have you heard from Becca and Cameron?"

"They're in the thick of things. Said they might need some help. I'm waiting on her call," Genie said and waved to the kids to come out.

"I hope they're okay," Cat said.

"I'm sure they are. Becca loves the action."

Cat grinned. "That's a fact."

"This place is incredible," Tom said, climbing out of the pool. He grabbed a towel from his chair and dried off, staring at the view of the ocean and Seattle across the sound.

"Does that mean you're going to stay?" Genie asked, and Cat held her breath, waiting for his answer.

"Believe me, it won't be as quiet as it appears," Genie continued. "SeaTak Airport is just a short ferry ride away for any ops you want to go on, or you can join us on ours. We don't deal with international drug dealers yet, but we've been known to tackle a terrorist or two."

"I've been thinking about it." Tom sat next to Cat. "I've really enjoyed these last few weeks here with you and the kids."

"With me, too?" Genie asked, handing him the tray of sandwiches.

Tom laughed and took one. "It's certainly never boring. Though it's a little scary watching Jayne start fires with her mind."

"Just don't get on her bad side," Genie joked.

Cat clutched her hands together, still waiting for him to give her his decision. Would he agree to uproot their lives, move across the country, and let her work with her sisters? And if he didn't? Would she break up her family and stay without him?

"Mommy, look," Mark yelled as he did a cannonball off the diving board. She gave him a thumbs-up sign when he surfaced. *No, her family had to come first. Always.*

"Time for lunch," she called to the kids. "Come on out."

"I've made some inquiries into the Seattle FBI field office. Just in case," Tom said.

"In case?" Cat sucked in a deep breath and bit down on her bottom lip.

"Oh, for God's sake, put us out of our misery and just tell us already," Genie cried.

"In case I get bored training agents here," Tom said. "Yes, let's move and give it a try. I've asked for a six-month leave. That should be enough time to decide if I want to stay with the CTA or go back to the FBI and work out of the Seattle office."

Cat squealed and threw herself into his arms. "I love you."

He hugged her tight. "I love you more."

"Me, too?" Genie asked, jumping to her feet and clapping her hands together as the kids climbed out of the pool.

"All of you," Tom said, laughing as their children flung themselves on them for a wet group hug. Cat's heart exploded with happiness. How on earth did she get so lucky?

"Who wants lunch?" Genie asked and handed the tray to the kids.

"We have so many happy memories in this house," Cat said as she watched her kids eat their sandwiches. "Now we get to make even more."

"Being near your family will be a wonderful thing," Tom said. "For all of us."

Cat leaned over and kissed him deeply. "Have I told you how much I love you lately?"

"Yes." He smiled. "But it's something I'll never grow tired of hearing because I love you, too, babe."

"Me, too," Genie said and hugged them both. "I can't wait for all of us to get started in our new venture."

The End

ABOUT THE DEADLY SECRETS SERIES

Thank you for reading **The Lies Between Us**, the fourth book in the **Deadly Secrets Series.** I love romantic suspense, especially the ones that have a psychic twist.

The Deadly Secrets Series offers high-octane romantic suspense that keeps you guessing until the very end.

A few decades ago, the Counter Terrorist Agency (CTA) started a program that studied, mapped, and enhance the sixth senses. They pushed ethical boundaries by experimenting on pregnant women. One of those women was Amelia Marsters. Her daughters, triplets, now work to help others like them, born with special abilities, and targeted because of them.

Some secrets are too deadly to share...with anyone.

ABOUT THE DEADLY SECRETS SERIES

DEADLY SECRETS LOVING LIES (Book 1)

Genie Marsters father, former head of the CTA, has disappeared, and she's the next target. She must find him, but first she has to survive. And find a way to work with her ex-partner, ex-lover...Kyle Montgomery.

Kyle's sure Genie betrayed him and their unit, almost getting him killed. Now, he's forced to work with her. She still makes his blood burn —in all the right ways. And she's still hiding things, this time, this secret, could be the most deadly weapon of all.

"Deadly Secrets, Loving Lies delivers a thrill ride of action-paced suspense." - Amazon reviewer

Buy Deadly Secrets Loving Lies Here

ABOUT THE DEADLY SECRETS SERIES

JOHNNY'S GIRL (Book 2)

Undercover agent discovers he's the prime suspect in the murder of his ex-girlfriend, and the cop investigating him is the woman he still loves.

Counter-terrorist Agent, Johnny Garino is hot on the trail of a deadly terrorist, until he gets a call. The body of his high-school sweetheart has been found in a mine on his family ranch and he is the number one suspect.

Small town cop, Gemma Connors doesn't believe Johnny, the boy she once loved, had anything to do with the death of their old friend, but after another body is found, it's clear they have a killer living among them. And he's not done.

This killer must be stopped and fast. Torn between his mission with the CTA and the woman he never stopped loving, Johnny has a choice to make and lives to save.

And he's running out of time.

Buy Johnny's Girl Here

BURIED SECRETS (Book 3)

Chet Daniels, newest member of the Counter Terrorism Agency (CTA) is trying to keep Jayne safe from a known terrorist, but she isn't making it easy. When fighting with Jayne becomes the highlight of Chet's day, he knows he's in trouble.

Unable to shake Chet loose, Jayne takes him to her childhood home hoping to discover why she's being targeted. The deeper she delves into her family's secrets, the more she fears there isn't anyone she can trust. Not her aunt, not the CTA, and not even the bodyguard who's stolen her heart.

Buy Buried Secrets here!

THE LIES BETWEEN US (Book 4)

A drug lord, a kidnapping, another woman—to save her marriage, Cat must fight them all.

Undercover FBI agent, Tom Phillips, is building a case against a known drug lord, but his confidential informant has disappeared. Tom's captured trying to rescue his CI and loses all hope until his wife does the unthinkable…

ABOUT THE DEADLY SECRETS SERIES

Cat's husband is missing. To find him, she must break her promise—hiding her extraordinary abilities is no longer an option. Tom's double life has put them all in danger. It's time he discovered who she is, and what she is capable of.

Buy The Lies Between Us here!

Coming in 2021

The subjects of the original Amelia Project will finally get their day, oh, and Becca will find a worthy love...

"The CTA would like you, along with some of the other subjects of the ISO 90 program, to come to work for them. To start a team, if you will, of agents with extraordinary abilities. If you think you'd be up for it, we could work together."
She looked up him, slightly confused.
"You want me to be a secret agent?"
"Yep. A crime fighting superhero."

Join my newsletter to stay updated on the next books coming out in the Deadly Secrets Series. Newsletter and/or follow me on Bookbub and Amazon. Or find me at: Website Twitter Facebook Pinterest

ABOUT THE DEADLY SECRETS SERIES

I hope you enjoyed this story, and if you have a moment, please recommend my book and leave a review at Amazon. The few extra seconds it takes are really appreciated. Thank you!

OTHER BOOKS BY CYNTHIA COOKE

For a complete list go Cynthia's Amazon Author page

Kiss The Bride Series

Book #1 - Going All The Way

Book #2 - All Night Long

Book #3 - All My Loving

Book #4 (Short) - All I Want Is You

A Pineville Christmas Series

Book #1 - Santa Claus is Coming to Town

Book #2 - Christmas to Remember

Book #3 Home for Christmas

Book #4 (Short) Candy's Christmas Rescue

Deadly Secrets Series

Book #1 Deadly Secrets Loving Lies

Book #2 Johnny's Girl

Book #3 Buried Secrets

Book#4 The Lies Between Us

Dark Enchantments Series

The Vampire's Reckoning

The Dragon's Woman

Coming Soon: The Vampire's Seduction

Bayou Secrets Series

Her Dark Lover

His Magic Touch

The Colony Series

Running With Wolves (The Colony Book 1)

Lying With Wolves (The Colony Book 2)

ABOUT CYNTHIA COOKE

First published in 2003, Cynthia Cooke is a USA Today Bestselling author who has published 30 novels in 12 different countries with Harlequin, Entangled, and Amazon Kindle Worlds. She has a deep affection for romance stories and playing in the ocean. On her best days you can find her on the beach with her notebook, a novel in hand, and her dog, Bella, by her side.

CYNTHIA LOVES to hear from readers!
Website: www.cynthiacooke.com
Email: Cynthia@cynthiacooke.com

Go to Cynthia's website to sign up for Cynthia's Newsletter to get latest news and exclusive content or click here-Newsletter Signup

Printed in Great Britain
by Amazon